Praise for

Perfect Timing

Kim Dare brings the best of BDSM and gay romance together in Perfect Timing: You First...When you want a BDSM book that really understands and brings the emotion you want You First.
~ *Two Lips Reviews*

You First is a scorcher of a read that reveals a softer side to the BDSM world...Buy yourself Perfect Timing: You First for a day you are in the mood for a smokin' hot read about love and lust!
~ *Joyfully Reviewed*

Kim Dare always delivers great stories and Time to Do is certainly no exception...Intertwining great conflict with equally as great characters seems to be her stamp. And I for one absolutely love this about her! ~ *Fallen Angels Reviews*

I loved it. Time To Do is securely on my keeper shelf, and I can't wait to see what this author writes next!
~ *Rainbow Reviews*

PERFECT TIMING
Volume One

You First

Time To Do

KIM DARE

Perfect Timing: Volume One
ISBN # 978-1-907010-97-2
©Copyright Kim Dare 2009
Cover Art by Natalie Winters ©Copyright 2009
Interior text design by Claire Siemaszkiewicz
Total-E-Bound Publishing

The author and illustrator have asserted their respective rights under the Copyright Designs and Patents Acts 1988 (as amended) to be identified as the author of this book and illustrator of the artwork.
Published in 2009 by Total-E-Bound Publishing Faldingworth Road, Spridlington, Market Rasen, Lincolnshire, LN8 2DE, UK.

Manufactured in the USA.

YOU FIRST

Dedication

To everyone who has ever had a stupid idea they
couldn't let go of, and especially to those who
were able to laugh at themselves while
they chased that idea.

Chapter One

Saturday

Luke Anderson was not going to come first.

He repeated the mantra over and over inside his head as he held his hands out to be bound. Justin Collins deftly buckled the soft leather around his wrists. Tugging on the chain between the cuffs, he positioned Luke on his hands and knees in the middle of the bed.

Justin attached the cuffs to a little hook screwed into the headboard for that precise purpose. He pulled at the chain, testing how securely it would hold Luke in place. The metal links clinked together. Luke took a deep breath. All his best sexual experiences occurred to that theme song. The sound went straight to his cock.

Luke was still not going to come first. He was Luke Anderson, newest and highest flying barrister in the best chambers in London. He could bloody well do anything he set his mind to.

Justin's hand applied pressure — a steady pressure to the back of his neck. Luke lowered himself onto his elbows. The pressure didn't ease. Luke turned his palms up and rested his head in his hands. Head down and arse up, Luke closed his eyes. He told himself for the thousandth time it must be possible.

Just because he hadn't outlasted Justin yet, didn't mean he couldn't do it. He just needed to focus. He was twenty-three years old — five years older than his lover. He'd topped and bottomed more partners than he could count or remember in both genders. False modesty and jokes aside, Luke was well aware he knew tricks even most really expensive professionals hadn't mastered.

He shifted his knees further apart on the mattress as Justin moved into position, kneeling on the bed behind him. He had to outlast Justin just once, just so he knew he could do it. Just for pride's sake, because Luke knew his lack of self restraint was the only thing that kept sex with Justin from being perfect.

Justin's fingers slipped briefly inside him, checking he was slick, relaxed and ready to play. Luke bit his lip and held back a moan as Justin crooked his fingers and found his prostate.

He could do this. Practicing a little bit of restraint wouldn't kill him.

The rustle of the packet when Justin slipped on a condom was his only warning. Justin slid into him in one smooth movement. Luke gasped. For a perfect moment, Justin stilled inside him, stretching him and filling him completely. He began rocking his hips, building up the movement in tiny increments. Only when Luke whimpered his frustration did Justin begin to thrust into him in earnest.

In what felt like moments, lethal frustration was a growing possibility. Each stroke pressed against Luke's prostate in a rhythm calculated to throw him over the edge at any moment.

He tried to remember he didn't want to fall into pleasure — why he didn't want to jump over the ledge with his arms spread wide in enthusiastic abandon. All he could think about was just how glorious it would feel when he came with Justin still buried balls deep inside him.

But still, in the back of his mind the mantra continued. Luke was not going to come first.

Desperately trying to concentrate on anything other than Justin's erection pounding into him, Luke scrambled for any other details and senses to focus on.

The cotton sheet underneath him was pale blue. At this angle, with his nose barely an inch from the surface, Luke saw it was actually two shades of thread blended together. He couldn't bring himself to care. His prostate sang inside him, coaxing him to join in with it in harmony, groaning his pleasure at every inch of delicious friction.

The scent of their arousal filled the room, mingling with Justin's aftershave. Justin always smelt fantastic. Another perfect thing to add to all the other perfect things Luke had noticed over the months they'd been hooking up for sex. He always smelt like old sandalwood and well worn leather. Luke loved pressing close against Justin's body and taking deep breaths of his scent when they danced together. He loved sliding his fingers up into Justin's hair and pulling him close, to wrap Justin's scent around him.

Luke threaded his fingers through his own hair. He pulled at the thick blond strands, hoping the pain might kill off some tiny bit of his arousal. The tug increased with each connection of Justin's hips against his arse. It did nothing to help his increasingly frantic desire not to come.

Justin's rhythm increased another notch. Cradling Luke's pelvis in his strong grip, he held him steady and absorbed part of the impact from each thrust. Luke rocked back with every motion. As he focused on the pressure of each fingertip against his skin, Justin's right hand left his hip.

He reached underneath Luke and started to jack him off with an expert touch. Luke pulled at the cuffs around his wrists. He couldn't reach down and push Justin's hand away. He had no choice but to accept the touch or say his safe word.

Luke clenched his internal muscles around Justin, desperately trying to milk the other man's orgasm out of him. If Justin didn't come soon Luke knew he would lose his grip on his control, his libido and possibly his every perception of reality along with it.

He just needed to hold on a little bit longer and…

And it was too late. Justin increased his speed, hit the perfect angle, and it was all over, for Luke anyway.

Justin thrust through Luke's orgasm, letting him enjoy every ecstatic moment while his muscles weren't entirely his own to control. Luke's come spilled on the sheet underneath him in time with each thrust.

Justin gripped him tighter, steadying Luke in the centre of the mattress and preventing a repeat of the Wednesday a few weeks ago when they fell off the bed. Luke always lost track of which way was up when he climaxed. Justin, of course, possessed perfect balance.

Luke eventually fell still. Almost like an afterthought—like he could have gone on for another ten minutes but he wouldn't bother because Luke was already done—Justin finished himself off with a dozen hard, deep thrusts. He gasped for breath, holding Luke's hips still as he filled him.

They stayed there, frozen in pleasure for a few wonderfully long moments. Luke tried to catch his breath. Those few minutes when neither of them had the coordination, the ability or the desire to separate their bodies were always amazing. He closed his eyes and savoured the sensation of Justin slowly softening inside him.

Justin moved first. He even had a quicker brain recovery time than Luke. That was adding insult to... it was adding insult to some of the best sex Luke ever had. Which actually wasn't that much of an insult when he thought about it logically. Shaking himself out of it, Luke moved too.

The chains on the cuffs rattled against the hook. Luke stared at them. With a mental shrug Luke left his hands where they were. He re-arranged the rest of his body around the limitations of the bondage and managed to avoid the sticky patch he'd created on the sheet. So, the coming second thing hadn't happened this time. It would happen next time. Next time, Justin would come first and perfection would begin in earnest.

Justin unbuckled the cuffs. While Luke shook his hands out of their hold, Justin stretched out on the other side of the bed. Pulling a pillow under his head, he settled himself just right. When he lifted one arm, Luke shuffled across the bed to lie curled comfortably against Justin's side.

He rested his head on Justin's shoulder. Justin pulled him closer. Murmuring contentedly, Luke let his eyes drop closed. In his experience, someone you could lie comfortably with after sex was even rarer than someone you could have good sex with. It took Justin's perfection to a whole new level.

Luke still remembered his disbelief the first time Justin pulled him close and encouraged him to rest against his body. Luke had waited for the punch line for a long time until he realised there wasn't one.

Guys did not cuddle with a casual hook up. There was probably a rule about it. But, realising Justin hadn't been informed of that particular rule, Luke found himself reluctant to expand the less experienced man's store of knowledge.

Justin sighed his sleepy satisfaction and pressed a kiss to the top of his head.

Luke smiled against his shoulder. Amongst his other varied talents, Justin was also a very comfortable pillow. He could happily lie in his arms for hours, but he would make do with staying there until Justin decided it was time to leave.

That was always Justin's decision. Luke never built up the energy to hint him towards the door after a polite period of time had elapsed.

"There's a new Italian restaurant on Hamilton Street."

Drifting in afterglow, Luke was quite content to believe Justin's random statement was accurate. "Is there?" He didn't make too much effort to pay attention. Luke liked afterglow. If he didn't think too much he could stretch it out and make it last for hours.

Silence descended once more.

"Do you like Italian?"

"Sure." Luke let the soft, easy sensations surround him again. Inside his brain, right at the back, in the place which during its evolution warned of spiders in the foliage and predators in night, a red flag waved frantically for him to pay attention.

Luke blinked. Other factors registered. Justin's contentment had morphed into tension. His muscles were knotted under Luke's sleepy caresses. His voice was a fraction to casual. He wasn't just resting. He wasn't even just cuddling.

"Are you asking me out on a date?" Luke asked carefully.

There were other explanations. He might just like talking about food after sex. He was very energetic. He could be hungry. Luke tried to remember what was in his fridge. There might be the makings of an omelette in there. He'd definitely seen eggs in there at some point, although he wasn't sure about the sell-by date.

"Yes, Luke. I am asking you out."

Putting the omelette idea aside, Luke tried to think quickly. People shouldn't ask complicated questions right after he came. It was inconsiderate to expect higher brain functions.

They'd never been on an actual date. They met at the club. They come back to Luke's place for sex. Sometimes they had a drink at the club first. Occasionally there was dancing. But they didn't date. They hooked up.

"Do you mean you want us to eat at the same table sometime, or do you mean you want us to *date*?" Luke asked carefully. Please just want to eat some time. He could easily do that without worrying about the implications or panicking about Justin expecting some sort of commitment from him.

"*Date*?" Justin copied the inflection precisely.

"*Date*. As in stop meeting up to have sex and move on to something different," Luke expanded.

"No."

Luke started to breathe again. There was no harm in sharing a meal. He'd been right to begin with. Justin was just hungry. Inviting Luke to eat with him was just a sign of politeness not seriousness.

"I definitely don't want us to stop meeting up or to stop having sex," Justin corrected. "But the eating at the same table, going to the cinema, conversations, they could all be good when added to the sex. Moving on to anything more than we have now should contain just as much sex as we have now—if not more."

Oh, so it was *dating* spelt with a capital R for relationship.

Luke considered his options. He'd tried dating when he was Justin's age and quickly came to the conclusion he wasn't a dating type of guy. He was much better at straight forward sex.

Still, putting Justin in the picture did add a certain shine to the idea. It would be nice to do other things with him — things which could conveniently fill in the gaps between the sex. It wasn't as if he couldn't stand Justin's company unless they were naked. And sometimes he did wish Justin would hang around just a little longer afterwards.

"I think that might work," Luke said carefully, "at some point in the future." Not straight away. One issue at a time. They were obviously still in the working out the chemistry and how to get each other off stage. When he'd worked out the stamina thing and was entirely sure he had their sex life where he wanted it, he would turn his attention to the dating thing.

"Cool." Justin nodded above him.

Silence descended again. Luke realised why this wasn't a conversation you should have with someone while you were naked in bed with them. Because afterward you had the conversation, you were still naked in bed with them. There was no way to avoid an awkward moment.

They lay in the silence for a while. Luke stared up at the ceiling. Dating could be interesting. Justin wasn't hysterical or psychotic, it would be a new experience for him to date someone who might qualify as sane.

Of course, if he didn't think of something to say soon, Justin would likely reconsider the whole idea, just when Luke was getting used to the prospect. If he couldn't make after sex conversation, what chance did they have spending a whole meal together?

The move was sudden, unexpected and put Luke flat on his back. Justin loomed over him. Luke gasped and instinctively tried to catch Justin's weight on his hands. Justin chuckled and pinned Luke's wrists to the sheet.

He leaned low over Luke. His breath tickled the strands of hair next to his ear. "Now, just because I know how to ask nicely once in a while, don't start thinking you'll be the one calling all the shots."

Luke swallowed.

"You won't be the one dating a submissive, Luke," Justin warned.

"I won't?" Luke cleared his throat. "You didn't sound incredibly dominant when you asked me out."

Justin's grip tightened on his wrists. "Don't mistake a submissive's veto for a dominant's control. If it's dating or sex, you get to say yes or no. Say no, and I'll respect that. But if you say yes, that's it. You belong to me, and you'll do as I say until I give you leave to do otherwise. Any questions?"

Luke shook his head. He flashed back to the first time Justin approached him at the club.

He'd been nice. He'd asked him to dance very politely. He'd also been very polite when he'd denied any of Luke's attempts to lead the dance. They danced as Justin wanted, or Luke could leave the floor and find another partner. They screwed as Justin wanted, or Luke could get out of bed and find someone else's.

"If you don't like the way I run my scenes, you'd best find a lover who is willing to satisfy your every whim, because I won't." Justin looked down at him.

"Do you like my way, Luke? Do you like knowing I'm in control? Do you like doing whatever I say?"

Luke licked his lips, trying to work some moisture into his suddenly dry throat. He nodded.

Justin, mere inches away from him, didn't seem to notice.

"I like it," Luke whispered. "I like knowing you're in control. I like doing whatever you say."

"You'll have to do better than parroting my own words back to me."

Luke couldn't meet Justin's gaze. He let his eyes rest on the side on Justin's neck where a lone freckle decorated the deeply bronzed skin. "I like it when you take all the little choices away from me."

Justin made him meet his eyes. His very expression demanded more.

"And I like you knowing how to ask nicely when you want us to do something new. I like feeling safe obeying your every command, because I know you don't command me to do anything unless you know it's within my limits."

"And do you think politeness makes me submissive, Luke?" Justin asked.

Luke shook his head. Leaning back, Justin smiled down. The grip on Luke's wrists slackened. It would have been easy to move his hands out of Justin's grip. Luke happily left them where they were.

"Soon." Justin's statement was halfway between the two personas Luke had come to know over the past months. Not polite enough to be a request, not dominant enough to be a demand, the word sounded more like an expression of hope.

There would be more than just sex between them soon.

"Soon," Luke agreed. He closed his eyes and arched into Justin's touch as Justin's hands left his wrists to trail over his skin.

Soon — about two seconds after Luke worked out how to get his cock back under his control and come exactly when he most wanted to — right after Justin.

* * * *

Wednesday

"Fetch the toy box." Justin's whispered words caressed Luke's ear.

Luke shivered at the possibilities the box contained. Crossing the room he pulled a large wooden box out from under his bed and undid the lock. He loved his toy box — he loved the sessions where Justin was inclined to explore its contents even more. Flipping it open, he stepped to one side and stood out of the way so Justin could make his selection.

"You've been shopping again," Justin observed.

Luke nodded. His newest purchases were placed conveniently on the top where Justin couldn't fail to spot them. A subtle hint that he would be very happy if Justin chose to pick those over the other toys.

"Close your eyes."

Luke did as he was told. His heart rate sped up. All the different things that could happen next, flashed across his imagination. A moment later something slipped over his face. Luke gasped. Blindfold? Hood? Something else? A length of smooth, caressing silk covered his closed eyes, blocking out any chance of sneaking a peek at whatever happened next. Justin knotted the fabric behind his head, careful not to catch his hair in the silk.

In his personal darkness, Luke heard Justin rummaging around in the box. Then he heard the shuffle of wood on carpet as the box went back under the bed. Luke took a deep breath. Justin had made his selection. The decision was made. Luke couldn't do anything to change that now—as if he ever had that chance.

"Stand up and strip."

Luke stood and briskly removed his clothes, dropping each item on the floor at his feet. The cool air of his bedroom brushed against his skin. When he was naked he lowered his hands to his sides and waited for further instruction. Tension raced through his body, knotting every muscle. He tried to listen for any clue as to what would happen next.

Nothing happened.

As he just stood there, still and silent, it began. Vulnerable and defenceless, Luke felt everything but Justin's presence drain out of his mind. The case he was working on, the hassles of the day, all the little things which lurked in the back of his mind in a never ending to-do list all faded from his consciousness.

Right here, in this moment, all he needed to do was obey. Life was simple and it revolved around Justin. The peace he never felt at any time descended. His breaths evened out and his lips twitched into a smile.

Justin's hands slid around his waist. Luke jumped. More strands of silk trailed over his body. Luke swayed blindly into each brief sensation. Justin walked in circles around his body. Silk caressed his neck, dropped down to brush across his chest—lower to tease his abs. Luke jerked forward. The material cocooned his cock for just a few seconds before swishing away and leaving him bare again in the cool air.

Justin took Luke by his right wrist and raised his hand in the air. Luke kept it in position when Justin let go. Justin tied the silk around it, leaving only enough slack to allow healthy circulation. He repeated the process with Luke's left wrist. He stood close behind Luke while he tied the fabric. His erection pressed against Luke through the layers of Justin's clothes. He was still dressed, then.

Luke didn't know why that knowledge always made him hot, but it inevitably did. He leaned back, eager to feel the roughness of clothing against his bare skin. The warmth of Justin's body behind Luke's back vanished. A length of silk trailed over his buttocks, flicking slightly in gentle imitation of a whip. Luke swayed towards it.

A touch to his calf told Luke that Justin now knelt behind him, binding him further. Silk wrapped snugly around each ankle, Luke tried to picture what he wasn't permitted to see.

He'd seen his body decorated by the black silk before. He was very fair skinned and Luke knew the contrast suited him very well. He didn't regret not seeing himself. But he wanted to see Justin. If he couldn't see then... He reached out, trying to locate his lover in the darkness.

"No."

That word in that tone of voice made him shiver. Luke dropped his hand to his side. The silk on his wrist swished against his leg.

"On the bed. On your hands and knees."

Luke licked his lips, working moisture into his throat. He stepped forward and found the edge of the bed with his shins. Carefully placing his hands on the bed sheet, he crawled onto the mattress. A sharp tug on each restraint put Luke exactly where Justin wanted him. Fabric rustled, not the distinctive sound of silk, but something softer, more like cotton on cotton.

"Down on your stomach."

Luke lowered himself onto the mattress. He found a pillow placed underneath his crotch, softening the mattress and tilting his arse up, offering it to Justin to do with as he pleased. Luke stretched his hands and legs out to each corner of the bed, guessing what would come next. He'd guessed correctly. Justin secured him in place, stretching him out until the there was hardly any slack in the fabric.

Bondage always pushed his buttons. Luke was already leaking against the pillow by the time he heard Justin shrug off his clothes. Justin quickly prepared him and slid inside. Luke pushed back against him as much as he could — it wasn't much.

Justin rode Luke hard and fast, as if he were only taking his enjoyment from Luke's body without any thought to the pleasure of the man beneath him. That thought alone made Luke whimper. Combined with the friction of the pillow against his swollen cock on every thrust, it was destined to be a short ride from the start.

Luke held on as long as he could. He tried to think cold thoughts, but the friction from his jerky movements made the silk warm against his wrists. Every increasingly frantic movement brought the bondage back to his attention.

Justin's body was hot above him, his breath scorching on the back of Luke's neck, his cock a column of burning pleasure inside him.

Luke came first. He scrunched his eyes up tight behind the silk, cursing himself for a fool. A few minutes later, Justin was finished too. He untied Luke and tossed the silk bondage aside. Luke reached for the blindfold. Justin's hand wrapped around his right wrist, where the silk had lingered until so recently. "I didn't give you permission to take it off."

Dropping his hand, Luke sat blind on the bed and waited for permission. It didn't come. Justin moved on the bed and led Luke to lie in his arms.

Aware of every sound in the darkness, Luke rested his head on Justin's chest and listened to the beat of Justin's heart under his ear. It sounded safe—steady and reassuring while the darkness kept him vulnerable. Luke opened his eyes behind the silk, for all the good it did him.

Safe—the kind of safe feeling which would only increase if he encouraged Justin to feel anything more than casual about him. Luke wriggled closer to Justin's side, enjoying the safety while it lasted. The silence stretched out.

More than leather, or chains, or silk, Luke felt bound by his decision. One issue at a time. Next time they lay replete they could discuss the relationship involving more than the sex thing. Luke would ensure they were on that issue by then.

Chapter Two

Saturday

"Do you work from home a lot?"

Luke nodded. Leaning in his study doorway, he watched Justin explore. There wasn't much for him to see. The room was what it was—a space where he worked. A few bookcases, a desk and the view out of the window. There wasn't anything interesting in the room unless someone had a fetish for legal text books.

With nothing better to do until Justin got their scene started, Luke admired the only interesting thing in his line of sight. Justin wasn't beautiful. He was too square jawed and long nosed to be pretty. But he looked just as Luke was sure a man should look—tall, dark and muscular—like someone who could go out and kill something edible if he needed to. Ridiculous considering Justin worked behind a desk in an advertising office every day, but there it was. He looked infinitely capable.

Luke shifted his stance, his cock swelling a little further with every minute he spent studying his lover. His eyes dropped down from broad shoulders to a perfect tight arse. Damn it, Justin had been in his apartment over half an hour and they were still both fully dressed. However hot he looked, that was just *wrong*.

He tried to keep quiet and tried to conceal his growing impatience. Justin was only making him wait because he got off on knowing he could, because he knew there was nothing Luke could do but put up with it. Luke held back a sigh and took some small comfort in the observation that he wasn't the only one tenting his trousers.

"Come here."

Justin stood on the other side of Luke's desk looking at the papers spread messily over the desktop.

Luke snapped out of his day dream and went to his side, wondering what Justin had seen of interest.

"Are any of these important?"

Luke glanced at the papers and shook his head. "No, why?"

"I want you naked."

It was about time. Luke turned toward the bedroom.

"I didn't tell you to leave the room."

Luke looked at the desk and back to Justin. He saw the look in the other man's eyes. Luke nodded. He began to take his clothes off, unable to drag his eyes away from his desk and what would come next.

As the last item of clothing hit the floor, Justin pulled him close and twisted him in his arms. In one easy movement he had Luke bent over his own desk. His papers crumpled underneath him. Justin's clothes rubbed against Luke's skin. His zipper scratched at Luke's leg as Justin thrust deep inside him and stretched him wide open.

Holding tight onto the far edge of the desk, Luke tried to pretend he hadn't whiled away a lot of boring office meetings picturing them in that exact position. He bit his lip, scrabbled at his paperwork and tried to remember the exact details of the Winchester account. Nothing could be less erotic than writing up briefs for that case. But even old Mr. Winchester was no match for Justin.

"One day we're going to have to have lunch at your office," Justin told him. Holding onto Luke's shoulder for leverage he delivered another hard thrust.

The desk shook.

Luke whimpered.

"I'll bend you over your desk just like this." Another thrust sent one of Luke's files spilling off the edge of the table to coat the carpet with legal terminology. "Stay nice and quiet now, or everyone in the office will hear you," Justin warned.

He took hold of Luke's left arm and twisted it up behind his back, as if Luke wasn't perfectly willing to stay right where he was and love every minute of it.

"If you don't come soon, you'll to be late for your meeting, Luke. All those fancy lawyers will come and see what's been keeping you. Don't think I'll stop just because we have an audience. You belong to me until I'm finished with you. Don't you ever forget that, Luke. You are mine until I give you leave to be otherwise."

The words shot down Luke's spine and lodged in his crotch. He squirmed on his desk. No matter how much he liked the sound of what Justin said, he couldn't let the words in completely without risking coming right then. Luke tried to pull his hand out of Justin's grip just for the joy of feeling it tighten. He murmured his pleasure at the strong hold.

"What's your boss's name, Luke?"

"Mr. Jennings," Luke whispered.

"What would he do if he walked in on us like this?"

Luke didn't even have to think about the answer to that. If Jennings walked in on him with a woman, maybe he'd stand a chance, but Justin? No way. "He'd fire me."

"Then you'd better come quick then hadn't you, you don't want Mr. Jennings to catch you taking it up the arse on your lunch hour?"

A knock echoed through the room.

Luke jerked. He threw his head back, looking frantically around the room. Justin thrust into him.

Luke's eyes dropped closed. He forgot about anyone but him and Justin existing and came in a sticky mess over his paperwork.

Only when Justin was finished and softening inside him did he manage to look up again and locate the door on the far side of the room.

No one was there. The doorway was empty. Luke frowned, trying to work out what was going on.

Justin tapped his knuckles on the desk next to him.

Luke chuckled in spite of everything. "Sneaky."

Justin pulled away and tidied himself up. Luke stood up, arching his back to work out the knots in his spine and shoulder. He looked down his body. His come had lifted half the ink off his paperwork. Patches of his cock and stomach were stained bright blue from the fountain pen notations he'd made in the margins.

"I've had blue balls before, but this is ridiculous," Luke muttered. He licked his fingers and tried to swipe the ink off his cock with his finger tips.

Justin laughed and led Luke through to the bedroom. Taking a wipe out of a packet on Luke's bedside table he tossed it across to Luke. He stretched out on the bed, still fully clothed and watched Luke clean himself up.

"On a similar note – did you have a good day at work?" Justin asked.

Luke shrugged. "Not bad." He tossed the now blue wipe in the bin by the bed. He hesitated then, not sure what Justin expected him to do next.

Justin tapped the mattress next to him. When Luke came to his side he wrapped his clothed body around Luke's naked form.

Luke cuddled close, taking comfort in the embrace. Justin was always very polite. If he noticed Luke's lack of self control, he never commented on it. Luke sighed into Justin's shoulder. This wasn't funny anymore. This was getting out of hand. He wondered if a man who had so little control over his own body could really expect to control a courtroom full of barristers and jurors at any point in the near future.

"You okay?"

Luke realised he'd stayed quiet for too long. "Just wondering how I'll ever work at that desk, at *any* desk, without a permanent hard on."

Justin chuckled.

Luke loved that full, rich sound. He smiled into Justin's shoulder. "If I get fired for sporting wood all day at the office, I'm going to blame you," he grumbled into Justin's shoulder. "And if I come in my pants next time someone knocks on my door, I'm going to sue you. I'm a really good barrister, you know, I could actually do that."

* * * *

Wednesday

"Are you saying I smell or something?"

Justin grinned. He shrugged the last of his own clothes off and started up the shower spray. Fiddling with the controls, he adjusted the dials until the water poured hot and pounding into the stall. It wasn't often Justin got naked first. Luke made the most of it and let his gaze linger.

The water ran over Justin's naked body, trailing intimate rivulets over hard muscles. The spray clung to the hairs on his chest and lower on the short thatch of hairs around his hard cock.

Suddenly, Justin pulled Luke under the water with him.

"Hey!" He'd only taken off his shoes and his coat. The water drenched his shirt. The thin cotton stuck to his torso, showing off the lines of slim muscle. His jeans soaked up the water in a matter of seconds, clinging rough and heavy to his skin.

Luke's back hit the tiles. His protest disappeared under Justin's kiss as Justin pressed him hard against the wall. Luke ran his hands over Justin's naked form, enjoying the play of muscles under his fingertips. His hands dropped down to Justin's arse. He cupped the tight globes of muscle and pulled Justin closer still.

Taking half a step back, Justin looked him over. He didn't usually let Luke stay dressed for this long. Luke pushed his sodden hair out of his eyes and waited for the command to strip.

"You look good wet."

Luke ran his eyes up and down his lover's body. "So do you." Justin looked like a Greek god rising out of the sea. Luke bridged the gap and kissed his neck. He half expected to taste the salt from the spray. Instead he tasted pure Justin.

If he couldn't win, Luke's legal training made it very clear that the appropriate response was to cheat. He dropped to his knees in the tight confines of the shower stall. There was no way Justin could out last him if he sucked him to the edge first.

Luke wrapped his lips around Justin's straining erection, glorying in the feel of the velvety skin against his lips. Justin was one of the very few dominant men Luke knew who rarely demanded a blow job, but as he stroked Luke's hair and wrapped his fingers tight into the wet strands Luke was sure it wasn't because he didn't appreciate them.

Even though Luke heard Justin's breath hitch and he tasted his pre-come leak onto his tongue, even though Justin was enjoying every moment, he didn't let Luke linger down there for long. After just a few minutes, he pulled him back up onto his feet.

Luke put his hands against Justin's chest. "Wouldn't you like me to suck your cock for a bit longer first?"

Justin met his eyes. For a moment, it seemed possible to sway him.

"I really love sucking your cock," Luke coaxed, looking up at Justin through his lashes in the way that worked with so many of his previous lovers. It wasn't even a lie. Luke had always liked going down on his lovers.

Justin turned him around. He put his hand between Luke's shoulder blades pushing him forward until he had no choice but to put his hands on the tiles or hit them head first. "When I want your mouth, I'll take it. Keep your hands there."

Braced against the white marble ready to be frisked, Luke stayed still. Even if his initial plan hadn't worked, he could still do this. Justin roughly pushed his soaked clothes out of the way. With his shirt open and his sodden jeans around his ankles, Luke hoped the muscle control required to keep him up on his feet might trigger better control of a few more personal muscles.

Luke arched his back, closed his eyes and waited for the blunt pressure against his hole. He didn't expect soapy hands sliding over his body. Justin's hands slid under his shirt, teasing his nipples. They instantly pebbled under his touch. Whenever the shirt got in the way, Justin just ignored it, soaping the cotton and Luke's skin alike. The scent of shower gel filled the room, mixing with the hot steam.

Justin's hand descended to Luke's cock. He spent several minutes just playing with him before he even reached for the lube. Wrapping his hand around Luke's erection, he stroked him quick and strong like a man possessed—like he was determined Luke should come before he even got inside him. Slamming his fist down to the root, he twisted on the upstroke and curled his fingers over the head, time and time again.

At that point Luke knew his chances were shot. He whimpered his frustration, squirming in Justin's grip, but never going so far as to pull away completely. He rested his forehead against the tiles and tried to hold himself back, but as he came, Luke was too relieved he hadn't embarrassed himself by coming before Justin even started to worry about the order of precedence right then.

When Justin turned off the water, Luke tried to take a step forward. The bondage of wet trousers still around his ankles made itself fully felt. He toppled backwards. Justin held him up, pulling him tight against his body until he was sure Luke had his balance back. Once he was steady, Justin helped him out of his wet clothes and dried them both off. A few minutes later they both collapsed in the bed mostly dry.

"Did you have a good day?" Justin asked, spooning cosily behind him.

Luke frowned at the wall opposite him. "Not bad. You?"

Justin said something. Luke nodded automatically but most of his brain was already devoted to working out just what scenario would let him outlast his lover and how to convince Justin to do that next Saturday.

Chapter Three

Saturday

Once the condom was on, Justin rolled onto his back against the pale green sheets. He pulled Luke on top of his body to straddle his waist. "Ride me."

Luke nodded. Relief flooded through him. This was his chance. Control of the speed and angle, had to help. Luke grinned to himself. That was the problem all along. It wasn't a matter of stamina, just dominance. He couldn't expect to out-last Justin when his lover was playing the dominant role. It would go against the submissive grain.

Luke closed his eyes as he lowered himself down and settled comfortably onto Justin's shaft. For a few moments, he stayed still, savouring the stretch as he adjusted to the intrusion. Very gradually he set up a slow rocking motion with his hips. From his experience in both positions Luke knew that particular sensation was far stronger for the mount than the rider. He could keep going like that all night, long after Justin spilt inside him, without ever coming close to the edge.

This was it. Everything would be fine after tonight. He dropped his head back, placing his hands on Justin's chest to steady himself as he took what little pleasure he could from the teasing pressure on his prostate.

Every muscle in his body clamped down around Justin's shaft. Luke's eyes flew open. "What the-"

Justin's hands were not as content to lie idle as the rest of him was. Luke automatically thrust into the tight channel between Justin's fingers. His one hand cupped Luke's balls, rolling the tight sacks between his fingers while the right hand slowly jacked him off.

"Don't be lazy, Luke. Move properly for me. That's right. I want you to thrust into my hand. Faster. That's better. Now put your hands behind your back and keep them there. I don't want them in the way while I admire the view."

Luke clenched his fists behind his back, grabbling for control as his nails bit into his skin.

"Open your eyes, Luke. Look down and see how pretty your cock looks in my hands."

He looked down. Those hands were going to be the death of him. He thrust up into the tight grip, watched the leaking pre-come smear over Justin's hands and slick his shaft. Dropping back down, he buried Justin's shaft further inside him. Justin filled him so much it was impossible to avoid his prostate. It was impossible to do anything at all while Justin's hands played as they did.

Sweat broke out on Luke's skin. His breaths came ragged.

Luke came first.

The only difference being on top made was, after he came, he had to keep moving until Justin caught up. His coordination wasn't too pretty by the end. Luke closed his eyes so he wouldn't have to watch it, wouldn't have to see the blush rise to his cheeks as he struggled to take his lover to completion.

Finally, Justin came.

Luke collapsed forward, resting his head on Justin's shoulder through the minutes as Justin softened and slipped out of him.

Luke was almost ready to give up and admit defeat, but by the time they lay curled up on their sides, Justin was ready to talk. His softly spoken words as much as his sleepily caressing hands, soothed Luke out of his embarrassment and his inclination to pout.

Justin didn't mention a date word again. The notion was planted in Luke's head and he seemed content to let it settle there for as long as it took to push Luke into action.

Luke smiled, listening with half an ear to Justin's voice while he day dreamed a little. Over the last few weeks Luke had found himself wondering more and more often where they might go on dates. He saw film trailers and wondered if Justin would like to go and see them. Eating out, he found himself scanning the menu and imagining what Justin would order if he was there.

The frustration was driving him insane. It was the only explanation. He had to be going insane, the only other explanation was he was getting soppy. In which case, insanity was the explanation to be devoutly wished for.

Luke smiled and nodded to whatever Justin said on general principle. Knowing the eighteen year old was able to outlast him was annoying. Realising how much he missed out on every time Justin walked out of his apartment without plans to do anything other than hook up for sex next week was actually far worse.

He had to do it. Just once. Like the last item on a to-do list which was never finished, it itched at the back of his mind. If dominance and control of the movement didn't work, he would have to think of something else that would. His pride wouldn't let him stay with a man who was better at sex than he was, and giving up Justin was unthinkable.

* * * *

Wednesday

Justin obviously wasn't in the mood for complicated. They closed the door to Luke's apartment behind them. Five minutes later, Luke was on his back. Justin put Luke's ankles to rest on his well muscled shoulders. Supporting his weight on his hands, he leaned forward, pushing Luke's flexibility to the limit until he was jack-knifed in half.

It didn't take Luke long to remember the missionary was classic for a very good reason. The position left his prostate wide open and Justin wasn't one to miss such an easy target on any thrust.

Luke dug his finger nails into the mattress and tried with increasing desperation to think of anything that wasn't erotic. Cold showers made him think of last Wednesday. Work made him think of Justin bending him over his desk. Everything only pushed him closer to his orgasm.

He took a deep breath and pulled out the big guns. The creepy security guard who worked in his apartment building worked for all of three minutes.

It almost worked too well. Luke felt his erection begin to wither at the thought of the red headed man who kept staring at him with such a scarily intent expression.

Justin's well timed hand around his shaft took him quickly back to full strength. If Justin noticed Luke's momentary lapse in stiffness, he didn't say so. His rhythm never even faltered.

Justin brought their mouths together, sliding his tongue into Luke's mouth and extracting a groan in payment for the kiss.

Luke lost himself in the contact until his orgasm caught him off guard. He didn't realise he was close to the edge until he was over the side and reaching back with his finger nails to cling on. Damn it, he was getting *quicker*!

Whimpering his frustration with his own lack of restraint, Luke turned his head to the side unable to met Justin's eyes. What the hell was wrong with him?

When Justin offered a shoulder to cuddle in, Luke wrapped himself tight against Justin's body.

"You okay?"

Luke nodded into his shoulder.

"You need to be a better actor if you want to lie to me, Luke."

Luke stroked his fingertips across Justin's bare chest, tracing imaginary lines around and around in circles down to his abs and back up again. He wasn't pathetic enough to actually admit why he was pouting.

"You seemed to zone out for a minute," Justin observed sleepily.

Luke tensed. There was no way he could let Justin find out about his project. Justin would *never* know he'd spent all this time jumping through stamina hoops for his benefit. He had to say something, anything to put Justin off the true trail. "I just had a strange thought, that's all." He left it at that, hoping it would be enough.

Justin jigged his shoulder where Luke's head rested. "Tell me."

How much of the truth could he get away with avoiding? All of it? "It was nothing."

Justin rolled them over so he looked down at Luke. "That's not an answer."

"Honestly?" A little bit of honesty couldn't hurt him. "There's this really creepy security guard on the night shift here. It's off putting when someone like that gets inside your head during sex. It just threw me off for a moment."

Justin stroked Luke's hair back from his face. "Is he hassling you?"

Luke smiled and shook his head. Justin really was sweet sometimes. "Don't get carried away Lancelot, he's just creepy. If I need a white charger, I'm quite a good rider myself."

Justin's lips twitched. "Yeah, last Saturday, I remember."

Luke grinned. "Yeah, well, you're not quite a horse." He looked down at Justin's cock—even flaccid he was impressive. "Although there are a few similarities…"

Justin laughed and Luke cuddled back into his shoulder. The moment of tension dissolved away like it never existed.

"Seriously, Luke, if he does become a real problem, you'll let me know?"

Luke leaned up on an elbow and looked down at him. Was that part of dating someone for more than sex? Most of his exes would have just asked if the guy was hot and suggested a threesome.

Luke saw the protective look in Justin's eye. He was really serious about this. Slowly he nodded. "If he's a problem, I'll let you know. I'll handle it myself," he added, because he was still capable of controlling any bit of his life that didn't contain Justin, "but after I've dealt with it, I'll let you know how it went."

Justin seemed vaguely content with that. Perhaps it was a step forward. The tension he'd been vaguely aware of building in Justin for some time disappeared altogether in that moment.

* * * *

Saturday

Justin wasn't there when Luke arrived at their hook up club. Luke shrugged, bought himself a drink and wandered around, wasting time until his dominant arrived on the scene. As he passed through the various rooms in the club, Luke nodded and raised his bottle of beer to old friends and old flames, often with little idea who fell into which category.

Studying his drink, Luke wondered how much he went through a night back when he was screwing his way through the local population. Not as much as some, and he'd stuck to the legal entertainments, but still.

Luke considered the shining glass cylinder carefully. Perhaps a little bit of drunk numbness might slow him down just enough. Maybe he always had a hair trigger and just been too drunk to notice? Luke shook his head. Damn, but he was getting pathetic.

Anyway, it wouldn't count. Maybe a few weeks ago he could have got away with cheating and lived with it. Not anymore. He needed to know once and for all that he could outpace Justin fair and square. Justin was important enough to play for keeps over.

Dropping the empty in a bin already half full of drained bottles, he went back to the bar. Would one more drink be cheating?

"It's bad luck to drink alone." A strong arm wound around Luke's waist, pulling him back against a hard chest.

Luke smiled. "Justin."

"You have to ask?"

Luke shook his head. It was a statement, not a question.

"I'll wait to have dinner with you," Justin whispered in his ear. "I'll wait until you're ready to admit there's more between us than sex. But if any man is this close to you, you'll know it's me. Won't you, Luke?"

Luke nodded and let his eyes drift closed. He was officially monogamous. That had to be the first time since he was legal. True, he hadn't actually taken another lover since he met Justin, but he'd kept the option open. In theory anyway. He'd known from the start Justin wouldn't have been impressed with the idea of him screwing around with anyone else.

"How many have you had?"

Luke blinked his eyes open. Surely the numbers conversation came after they started eating dinner together!

Justin chuckled and kissed his neck. "How many beers have you had?"

"Oh, just the one… beer," he clarified.

"Good, I want you sober. And I do want you, Luke." His hand dropped low onto Luke's stomach and pushed him back so his arse pressed tight against a flourishing erection barely restrained behind Justin's jeans.

Luke nodded.

"Now," Justin added.

Luke tried to remember how to do something other than nod as Justin started to rock his hips behind him. He failed, but apparently a verbal answer wasn't required. Justin was ready to leave. He led the way through the club and out into the parking lot, barely looking over his shoulder to check that Luke was there.

Luke followed, as Justin knew he would, until he relaxed back in the passenger seat of Justin's beaten up old sports car. It wasn't far to Luke's place. The guard on duty in the garage under Luke's apartment block knew Justin's car better than he knew Luke's. He let them in with a nod and a friendly wave.

Justin glared at the guard. Luke suppressed a smile. He wondered if he should point out the man on duty that night wasn't actually the guard he found creepy.

Luke whiled away the elevator time trying to guess what Justin would be in the mood for. Luke always tried to guess. He always got it wrong. Justin's moods were impossible to read.

As Luke opened the door to his apartment, he didn't expect anything specific. He could be pinned against the wall before Justin even shut the door behind them. Or Justin might make Luke wait for ages just to drive him mad with frustration, like he had not so long ago in his office.

Justin was a different mood again that night. The kiss in the hallway was almost chaste. Justin sweetly brushed their lips together, as if it was a first kiss, an initial taste of a mouth he'd fought to claim. Seeming to savour the gentle contact, Justin refused to cooperate when Luke tried to dirty up the kiss.

Keeping it a tease, closed mouths brushing together again and again, Justin made an inclination for a real kiss into a craving.

Luke tried every tongue slick trick he knew to push Justin to progress. He didn't object to screwing in the hallway, but Justin's gentle kisses left him stupidly out of his depth. They made him realise all over again how much he was losing by keeping their relationship solely sexual and entirely casual.

Gentle kisses gave a hint of the man behind the dom. They made Luke wonder what it would be like to fall asleep in Justin's arms only to be roused in the middle of the night by those same kisses if Justin woke up from a sexy dream with a hard on.

Justin led the way slowly to Luke's bedroom. He ceased the kisses, but he wouldn't let a rush take their place. Luke looked down at their joined hands.

Justin could always take Luke with him into whatever mood he occupied. With Luke in his most lethargic of tempers, Justin would make him crave the same high energy acrobatics he desired. When Luke practically bounced off the walls with pent up desire, Justin somehow made slow, controlled sex the exact compliment to it.

In the bedroom, Justin drew the curtains across the huge picture windows and switched on a lamp next to the bed. With the shade tilted as it was, it barely provided definition to the shapes and corners of the furniture.

Justin turned his attention back to Luke. Not one to fumble with fastenings, he soon had him standing naked in the middle of the room. He allowed Luke to return the favour, slowly dropping each item of his clothing to the floor around them.

Guiding Luke with soft caresses, he positioned him on the bed.

Stretched out on the satin sheets, Luke tried to get the party started. Justin replaced Luke's hands on the slippery black material. Bondage was nice, but not strictly necessary for the submission he enjoyed so much to take hold.

Luke knew to keep his hands flat on the sheet until told to do otherwise. He knew that Justin was serious about it too. If Luke took his hands away, everything would stop. Justin was in control and Luke couldn't mess with that.

Luke couldn't think of one corner of his body that Justin hadn't memorised over the months, but he went over each inch of him again. Stroking his skin, Justin coaxed nerve endings to plead for his attentions and ignored the obvious in favour of the neglected. Luke wriggled under the caresses, trying to hold himself back even at that early stage, so he'd have a better chance later on.

While his erection inevitably attracted its fair share of stimulation, Luke hadn't realised how sensitive the skin behind his knees was — or how lapping kisses could drive him crazy when they concentrated there for an unreasonably long time. He didn't realise that Justin knew his body and his reactions better than he knew them himself.

From the small scar behind his right ear to the birthmark under his left foot, Justin's careful attentions drove him crazy. And Justin hadn't done anything Luke considered to be real sex yet. Hard and leaking pre-come onto his nice clean sheets, Luke tried to recite sports stats in his head. He couldn't think of more than three football teams and he didn't care how they played.

Finally, Justin lost interest in teasing and positioned Luke on his side to spoon behind him. Luke took a deep breath. Staying the night was certainly an acceptable activity for someone who was dating. And the idea of them both falling asleep right there afterwards and in exactly that position, appealed to every fibre in Luke's body.

Confident Justin would look favourably on an offer to stay the night, Luke only needed to come second to be wholly in favour of it himself. He wanted it so badly he could taste it with every breath he took.

Stroking the lube inside Luke, Justin took the opportunity to tease a little further. Luke thought about penguins in the Antarctic, his old math teacher in her underwear and the humiliation of coming first again.

Eventually Justin was satisfied with his preparations. Slicking his condom covered erection with more lube, he positioned himself tight to Luke's back and rocked his way into his body in frustratingly tiny increments.

Luke was on the edge by the time Justin took up a rhythm, thrusting slowly, making sure Luke felt every inch of his shaft inside him. One fist crept around and took Luke in hand, Justin began to kiss his neck, high up next to his ear where he was most sensitive and where it was most convenient to whisper his compliments.

Mindful of Justin's earlier instructions, Luke's hands still rested on the bed sheet. If he could just reach out and move Justin's hand off his cock everything would be so simple. His fingers curled into the material, scrambling for his control. Justin continued to whisper. "You feel so amazing, Luke, so tight and hot around me. So perfect."

And everything would be perfect with Justin, Luke was sure it would. All he had to do was not come and perfect was right there waiting for him.

"Come for me, Luke."

Luke shook his head. He was not going to come.

Behind him, Justin's attitude changed. "You will come when I tell you to or I might not let you come at all." Justin thrust harder into him, massaging his prostate until Luke's fingers ripped the sheet.

The submissive inside him screamed. It struggled against Luke's self control, demanding to be freed to do what his dominant wanted. Somehow Luke held back. He pushed the instinct down and shook his head again. Justin was close to his climax. He could hear it in his lover's voice, feel it in the breaths he took and the air dragging against his shoulder. Justin was almost there — even he couldn't last forever.

Eventually, when Luke was almost ready to give up hope, Justin's rhythm faltered. One thrust, another. He came deep inside Luke.

Luke closed his eyes savouring the moment of perfect bliss before he fell into another one of his own creation.

Justin's hand squeezed tight around Luke's cock.

Luke gasped and tried frantically to extract himself from Justin's grip. He only pushed himself back harder against Justin's still pulsing cock. Luke made a weak little noise of protest in the back of his throat. Kinky was one thing, that bloody well *hurt!*

A moment later, Justin's grip eased. He pulled away and deftly dispensed with the condom as if nothing unusual had happened.

The squeeze hadn't been hard enough to soften Luke completely, just enough of a shock to stop him from coming that instant. Trying to pull his thoughts together, Luke guessed it was the product of some unconscious muscle movement when Justin came and it would probably be best not to make a fuss about it.

He would have preferred to come with Justin still buried inside him, but Luke would take what he could get. He would think more clearly for their imminent conversation if he wasn't drowning in frustration. Luke wrapped his hand around his cock.

Justin grabbed his wrist. "No. I gave you a choice. You didn't come when you were told. Now you wait until I repeat the command. You will not touch yourself. You will not come. Do you understand?"

Luke nodded mutely. Not getting off this one time wasn't so big a price to pay for his success. And Justin wasn't sadistic enough to leave him hanging for long. Luke had every confidence he would come before Justin left the apartment, even if it meant waiting until tomorrow morning after Justin stayed the night for the first time.

That sounded good. Luke took a deep breath and stared at the ceiling. He tried to resist the temptation to grin. He did it. He didn't even cheat and he came second. He'd made the timing perfect, adding that last bit of perfection they needed in their sex life. Luke Anderson was back on form and he rocked!

Justin lay watching him. When the silence stretched out for several minutes Luke finally brought his mind to consider something other than his own self satisfaction. He wondered if he was imagining the undercurrent of tension in the room. Justin didn't usually waste time before encouraging him close. Luke glanced at him, trying to work out what he was thinking.

Justin studied Luke's flourishing erection, deep in thought.

It was obviously one of those times when Luke didn't have a say in the details. He waited for Justin to say something. He didn't. Justin reached out and ran gentle fingertips over Luke's cock.

Instinct took over. Luke thrust into the contact.

"Stay still!" The command cracked like a whip in the silence.

Luke stilled, every muscle in his body froze at that tone of voice.

Justin went back to petting his cock. He watched his own actions intently, as if he just discovered a new and interesting species of beetle under a rock and wasn't quite sure what he thought of it yet.

Luke tried to stay still. He couldn't hold back a whimper.

"Do you want to come?" Justin asked casually.

Luke forced himself to be polite rather than sarcastic no matter what the provocation. "Yes."

Justin raised an eyebrow.

Luke managed not to roll his eyes. "Yes, I do want to come." He thought about throwing a "sir" in there for good measure, but decided it was safer to stay silent. If Justin wanted an honorific he would order one.

"That's greedy, Luke," Justin said. The disapproval in his voice wasn't over emphasised like it usually was when he teased. He sounded serious.

Luke swallowed down a sudden rush of nerves.

"I gave you the opportunity to come a few minutes ago," Justin reminded him. "You didn't take it."

Luke didn't know how to explain it without sounding like an idiot. Okay, he was willing to admit to himself that he was an idiot. But sounding like one would spoil the moment. And the moment was too important to be wasted. He needed to get the perfection going properly right now.

"You didn't want to come with me inside you," Justin observed coldly.

"No!" Damn, why hadn't he thought about how it would look to Justin? "That wasn't it. I really wanted to. You have no idea how hard it was for me to stop myself like that!" he babbled.

"So, you were holding back from me?"

In hindsight, it probably wasn't the most submissive thing to have done. But it was a hell of a lot better to confess to that than to let Justin believe he wasn't enjoying himself. "Yes," Luke admitted.

"Why?"

Luke broke eye contact and studied the sheet. The truth wouldn't come to his lips. Why, wasn't the important question anyway. Luke only had to make sure Justin knew everything was fine between them. Justin wouldn't really care about some stupid idea of who came first—it was really best not to mention that bit of silliness.

"It wasn't anything you were doing," Luke started to explain carefully.

"It wasn't me—it was you?" Justin swung away, to sit on the edge of the bed. "If you're going to say you want us to stay friends, at least save it until we're dressed."

He grabbed his clothes up off the floor and got dressed faster than Luke had believed physically possible. Jeans on in three swift movements, Justin barely bothered with anything else. Snatching his shirt and his shoes from the bottom of the bed, he left the rest on the floor.

The bedroom door swung open before Luke could really believe he was leaving. By the time Luke reached the bedroom door, he heard the apartment door slam shut. He raced after Justin.

Halfway down the public hallway he realised he was still bare arse naked. "Shit!"

He rushed back into his apartment before anyone could report him for indecent exposure. The way his luck was running the creepy security guard would turn up to perform a citizen's arrest on him any moment. If he'd picked his own trousers on the way past, he might have caught up. Although the pace Justin strode at, he would have had to sprint all the way. Now Luke knew he'd lost his chance.

Trailing back to the bedroom, Luke slumped on the bed.

The bed looked big. It was big. But it never seemed too big for one person before. He really didn't want to sleep alone there tonight. He looked around his room, a frown marring his forehead.

His erection might not have flourished through the whole argument, but Luke was still half hard. There was no reason not to finish off now. Except Justin told him not to. He didn't have permission to come. Luke guessed he should try to be on his best behaviour until Justin forgave his perceived disobedience.

Sighing, Justin snatched a pillow from the top of the bed and held it over his face, hiding from the world. It smelt of Justin's after shave. Luke took a deep breath, filling his lungs with the memory of his lover. It would be a long time until Wednesday and Luke's next chance of seeing Justin at the hook up club.

Chapter Four

Wednesday

After work, Luke raced home for a shower and change of clothes. Then he was straight off to the club. He was waiting outside when the doors opened. Ignoring the strange look from the barman, he ordered beer before changing his mind and ordering a coke.

Justin hadn't been too impressed with him drinking alcohol last time. If he wanted Justin to take his apology seriously, he had to show he could learn from his mistakes. It wouldn't hurt to have their conversation sober either.

Unable to sit still, Luke wandered through the rooms as they started to fill with leather clad revellers. Nodding and waving to the friends who shouted greetings, he kept moving. The last thing he wanted to do was stop and talk. The way his luck was running that would be the exact moment Justin would turn up.

And he would of course assume he was chatting some other guy up and screwing around behind his back.

Luke paced back and forth around the club, constantly scanning for a head of dark hair over the top of the crowd and rehearsing what he was going to say inside his head. Once Justin was willing to talk, he would explain how he'd developed some stupid notion in his head. Somehow he would avoid the details of what exactly that notion was. Then Justin would forgive him. He might make him jump through a few hoops first. That was to be expected, but Luke also expected to enjoy every moment of it. Justin might like to play games and play the dominant, but he'd never really punished him before. It was doubtful he'd start now.

Unlike any of his previous dominant lovers, Justin was always meticulous about making sure Luke enjoyed everything they did together. Luke sighed. Maybe it was just one of Justin's kinks—he liked to get submissives off. Luke took control of the decision. No wonder Justin was pissed.

"Can I buy you a drink?"

Luke barely switched his brain out of neutral. "Thanks, I already have a drink." He held up his full glass of coke as proof but didn't bother to look over his shoulder. He'd recognise it if it was Justin's voice and he didn't care who else it was.

The presence he felt behind him didn't leave.

Luke turned. His creepy security guard stood behind him. Luke forced a smile.

The security guard smiled back. "Are you here with someone?"

"I'm meeting someone."

"It's pretty late. Don't you think it's time to consider the possibility he stood you up?"

Luke shook his head. "I'm sorry. Even if he did, I'm still with him. Justin and I are exclusive." The words were out of his mouth before he thought better of them. They were a lot easier to say than he ever expected. There was no uncomfortable feeling in the pit of his stomach, no feeling that saying those words forced him to miss out on something better than he had, and Luke didn't think that was just because the security guard was doing that creepy staring focus thing again.

"The guy who keeps driving you home?"

Luke nodded. Where was the line between creepy and stalking?

The guard smiled. In spite of everything, Luke noted was kind of cute in a psychotic sort of way. "I just won fifty quid."

Luke blinked at him.

"I know the security staff shouldn't take bets on the residents, but I just knew you two were more than friends."

Luke closed his eyes. "You had a bet on me?"

The guard nodded. "Um, you're not going to report us or anything, are you?"

Luke shook his head, relief ringing through him. "No. But a bit of free advice?"

The guard nodded and waited to hear it.

"I was two creepy moments away from getting a restraining order on you. You want to take bets, take some lessons in subtlety first."

The guard laughed. "Will do. Oh, and if you could happen to subtly let Tommy from the night shift know you're gay and screwing the guy who keeps driving you home, it would really help me out. Fifty quid is fifty quid — you know?"

"I'll see what I can do," Luke promised. The guy walked off. Luke watched him go. He shook his head again. At least that was one less thing to worry about. Now his only problem was Justin.

Other guys approached him. Luke gave them all the same polite brush off. He was meeting someone there. By the early hours of the morning, Luke still couldn't admit to himself or anyone else that Justin wasn't coming. He stayed until the bouncer locked up at the end of the night.

Sitting in a taxi on the way home, Luke decided Justin's failure to show was nothing to worry about. Sometimes Justin couldn't make it on Wednesdays. He generally mentioned it the previous Saturday if that would be the case, but it might have slipped his mind with everything else and his sudden departure.

Luke wrapped his arms a little tighter around his torso. It was nothing to worry about. Even if Justin avoided the place on purpose, it wasn't serious. Justin only wanted to show him who was boss. Justin was the dominant. He set the rules. He set the time table. Luke shouldn't mess with it.

It was probably a punishment too. Justin had made it very clear Luke wasn't allowed to jack off without permission. Skipping a hook up night was a way of keeping him frustrated until next Saturday. If Justin liked getting his submissive off but wasn't inclined to let Luke enjoy himself right now, missing a hook up was the obvious way to punish Luke while not punishing himself.

Walking into his building he waved to the security guard on duty. As much as he would like to help the not so creepy after all security guard out, he first had to find Justin and convince him to cooperate.

Luke lay alone in his bed, staring up at the ceiling and repeating to himself over and over again that he was no longer a teenager. It wouldn't kill him to go a few days without getting off. Frustration wouldn't actually be fatal.

Luke sighed and turned over. It was his own fault for being a slut for so long. He wasn't used to showing restraint either with a guy or when he was on his own. Luke battered his pillow, trying to convince it to take on the shape of Justin's shoulder. It wasn't the same.

Luke looked at his alarm clock and wondered at what point it stopped being pathetic to start counting down to Saturday night?

* * * *

Saturday

If the days leading up to the Wednesday were long, then those leading up to the Saturday stretched out to the horizon and back again. Luke kept checking his watch to make sure it hadn't stopped, flicking over pages in his diary because he was sure it couldn't still be Friday. Keeping his hands away from his cock wasn't helping. But more than not getting off, not seeing Justin was driving him slowly crazy.

Luke wanted his dominant. Almost as much as he wanted to get off, he wanted Justin to hold him close the way he always did after sex and tell him he was pleased with him and all was forgiven.

The line between what he wanted and what he needed began to blur. He *needed* Justin.

He was there when the club doors opened again. Just when he was starting to wonder if Justin would turn up at all, Luke finally saw him on the other side of the dance floor. Taking a deep, relieved breath, Luke moved across to the bar where he would be easily spotted and settled down to wait.

Justin glanced in his direction. Luke was sure he'd seen him, but Justin didn't cross the dance floor. He turned back to the man next to him as if he didn't know or care Luke was there.

Luke waited.

Justin was obviously having a good time. He laughed and talked to all the men in his group, Luke couldn't help but notice one man in particular received a great deal of Justin's attention. Attention which should rightly be his.

Luke narrowed his eyes and studied the man hitting on Justin. He was deeply tanned and dark haired. Tall and handsome, he had large soulful eyes that Luke knew, even from his distant vantage point, would be stunning when he turned them up to flirt with Justin through ridiculously long lashes.

Justin was making him wait on purpose. Luke didn't doubt it. He didn't like it either. It was nothing like those times in his apartment. That was fun in a frustrating way, there was never any chance Justin would go home with someone else when he was already in Luke's place. Luke squirmed on his bar stool, fighting down the urge to cross the room and remind Justin he existed and they were supposed to be bloody well monogamous.

When Justin finally turned towards him, Luke braced himself. Justin was evidently still pissed with him. He had a lot of ground to make up. But he looked forward to making up each inch, very slowly and with a great deal of friction on every inch. Luke's eager anticipation drained away when he realised Justin was bringing the other man with him. A threesome wasn't out of the question in the long run, but not tonight... no, not tonight.

Justin and his new friend stopped in the middle of the dance floor.

From firsthand experience, Luke knew Justin was an amazing dancer. He could have Luke hard and aching in moments when he led them to thrust together again and again to the beat of the music. Luke felt himself sway with the music, trying to follow Justin's moves from across the room as if he was in his arms.

Justin didn't even try to put any space between him and the man with the puppy dog eyes. For a brief moment, Justin looked straight at Luke. Luke dropped his eyes in instant submission. A few moments later Luke forced his gaze back up. Justin still watched him, his expression cold and detached.

They writhed together on the dance floor for ages. Justin would have had his balls on a platter if Luke let another guy rub himself all over his body that way. Luke bit his tongue and pushed down his jealousy until Justin finally disentangled himself. Stopping at the bar, barely a few feet from Luke, Justin ordered a drink.

Luke waited with false patience to be recognised.

Justin took his drink from the bar and turned away, as if he really would pass by without a word.

Luke stood up and put his hand on Justin's arm, desperation making him break all the rules and make the first move.

Justin looked at his hand.

"I know you're mad at me, but can we at least talk?" Luke asked.

"What do you want to say?"

Luke hesitated. He was good with words—his job demanded it, but his mind went blank and he couldn't think of anything Justin would like the sound of.

"Exactly, there's nothing to say."

"So that's it?" Luke demanded, anger welling up and pushing his submission aside. "I make one mistake and that's it?"

Justin closed the gap between them, stepping right into Luke's personal space. The movements of the air brought the familiar scent of his aftershave. It had faded from Luke's pillow almost a week ago. He'd missed it over the last few days. Luke took a deep breath and savoured its return.

"If you stopped getting off on us, I could accept that," Justin snapped. "But you didn't, Luke, you stopped *wanting* to get off on us. If you lost interest you could have just said so. You didn't have to provide me with a show and tell demonstration."

Luke shook his head. "It wasn't like that…"

"Just forget about it," Justin turned to walk away.

"Justin…"

Justin sighed and turned back to face him again. "It was fun for a while, it didn't work out. No hard feelings," he muttered.

"Wait, I…" Luke just couldn't get his words out.

"Luke!"

The words were delivered with so much force, Luke took a step backwards. He'd never seen Justin mad — dominant yes, but not genuinely furious. Justin closed his eyes for a moment. When he opened them he was visibly calmer.

"I'm trying to be reasonable," Justin said quietly. "I'm trying to be a nice guy about this. You lost interest. You dropped enough hints over the last few weeks. I didn't pick them up until it was too late. Maybe it's a submissive thing. You found it easier to act out than just say no to me. I don't understand that, but I've accepted it. But, damn it Luke, I was half way to falling in love with you. So right now, I'm asking you to give me my space and you should be able to respect that request."

He was half a dozen steps away when Luke grappled for any words at all. "I always come first," he blurted out.

The words were too loud. Several people turned to stare at him, but Justin turned around once more and that was all that mattered.

"What?" Justin obviously didn't know what he was talking about, but at least the confession brought him back to Luke's side.

Keeping his voice low, Luke knew he had no choice but to confess properly. "You're eighteen and I'm twenty three. I have been having sex for over half a decade. There is no way you should be able to last longer than me *every single time*." Well aware he sounded like a two year old having a tantrum, Luke still couldn't keep a trace out the pout out of his voice.

"You... because I... you just wanted me to get off first?" Justin asked. Luke watched him struggle to wrap his mind around the concept. He'd never heard Justin falter over his words before.

"Yes," Luke snapped. He felt the heat rise to his cheeks. If he really had to have this conversation then so be it, but having it in the middle of a club full of his friends and former lovers added a special brand of torture to the event. Justin kept his voice down. No one could over hear. Luke still saw them all around him and felt his skin crawl.

Justin considered him carefully for several moments. "It really bothers you?"

"No," Luke said automatically. He sighed, the truth really sucked. "Maybe a bit." He looked over his shoulder.

Justin took him by the wrist and led them through the crowd until he found a quiet spot in a dead end corridor. He turned Luke and backed him up against the wall.

That was promising. Luke looked up at Justin's face. The dom was back full force in his eyes. There was something else, too. The anger had faded away to be replaced by a softer, warmer emotion. A fair bit of lust lurked in the pupils too. Lust was always a good sign in Luke's book.

Justin's hand stroking him through his leather trousers was an even better sign.

"Do you touch yourself like this?" he asked softly against Luke's ear.

Luke shrugged. "Of course...sometimes." He wasn't going to admit he'd followed Justin's instructions to keep his hands to himself unless he asked a direct question or threatened him with a harsh punishment—like not being allowed to come in the next ten minutes.

"Today?"

Luke shook his head. Apart from the temporary instinct towards excessive obedience, why the hell would he bother with his own hand when he expected to see Justin at the club?

"Do you ever, on the days we met up?" Justin asked, his fingers still stroked through the thin leather, outlining Luke's erection, coaxing him harder.

Luke shook his head again. He still wasn't sure where Justin was going with this and his hand was rapidly making it difficult to care.

"Do you think that might have something to do with it?"

Luke frowned and tried to pull his brain back up above his belt. "I'm not some teenage boy who has to jack off before a date so I can..."

He looked into Justin's eyes, saw the amusement there. Dropping his head back against the wall with a thud, Luke got it. "You do."

"Yes." Justin grinned, obviously very comfortable with that fact.

"I don't understand," Luke complained.

Justin smiled at him and dropped his eyes, not in submission, but to enjoy the sight of his hand against Luke.

Luke put a hand on Justin's wrist. He couldn't think while he did that. Justin stopped stroking but merely changed to cup Luke instead. His hand was wonderfully warm. It took all of Luke's control not to thrust into the welcoming heat.

"I usually jack off in the shower before I leave the house."

"Why?"

Justin chuckled. He met Luke's eyes without any trace of embarrassment. "Because I'm eighteen and I don't want everything over in as many seconds."

Luke hesitated. If that really was the case then... "Maybe you don't need to get off before we meet up."

"Unless you intend to get bad at sex any time soon, I do. Come on, you're not modest enough to deny you know you really are that good." He made Luke meet his eyes. "I want what we do to be good for you too."

"It is," Luke said quickly. He remembered the look in Justin's eyes when he hadn't come. The idea he couldn't please his submissive was just as hard for Justin as it would be for Luke to think he wasn't able to please his dominant.

Choosing his words carefully, Luke said, "What I meant was, maybe you don't need to get off before you meet me. You could still get off before you top me if you still wanted to."

Justin just looked at him like he was waiting for a translation.

"You wouldn't prefer my hand to your own?" Luke asked with a slightly teasing tone. "Or my mouth?" He paused to let Justin consider the prospect. "You wouldn't like me to get you off on my knees first. And then make me work to get you hard again before I had any chance of coming with you buried balls deep in my arse?"

Justin stroked across Luke's lips with his thumb, back and forth, over and over again. Luke's eyes drooped and he flicked his tongue out to lick the digit.

When his eyes fluttered back open Justin was watching him with obvious appreciation.

It wasn't a perfectly private location, but Luke had made do with a lot worse in the past. He was too aroused to be fussy. Still bracketed between Justin and the wall he lowered himself to his knees. Justin let him descend, but once Luke was there he titled his face up and just stared at him for a long time. Luke swallowed and tried to look away.

The conversation left him feeling vulnerable in a way sex never did. He wanted his safe territory back again. He reached for Justin's fly, but his hands were moved aside. Justin was just as eager for it as Luke was. From his current point of view, Luke could hardly fail to notice that Justin was up for what he was offering.

Justin pulled him back up to his feet.

Anal here against the wall was more complicated, but Luke was willing to give it a go. He would have done anything right then.

"I'm sorry."

Luke blinked. In his experience dominants received apologies, they didn't issue them. "For what?"

"I obviously failed to provide the sort of structure you need."

Luke swallowed. The tone of voice was enough to make it difficult to concentrate on the meaning of the words.

"I've been far too lax in your discipline."

Luke shook his head. The teasing note in Justin's voice reassured him nothing was really wrong, but the words didn't make sense. He couldn't work out what Justin wanted from him and that scared him.

"I…"

"Hush," Justin soothed. He kissed Luke very gently on the lips. It was brief and chaste and over before Luke could even part his lips in invitation. Licking at his lips and trying to gain any taste of his lover's mouth, Luke obediently hushed.

"You need more rules, don't you, sweetheart."

Luke shook his head. He parted his lips only to be shushed again.

"I asked you before if you wanted more than sex with me. I want a proper answer this time."

"Yes," Luke whispered, "I want more."

"Good. From now on, you won't worry about who comes when or where or how. You will come as and when I tell you to do so. If you don't come on command, you will be punished. If you come at any other time, you will be punished."

Luke tried to sieve the words through his brain but they went straight to his cock and lodged there making him swell further until he ached. Luke shook his head. He wanted to clear it rather than refuse, but as a tiny portion of his mind made sense of events he realised he was in the middle of a negotiation and didn't know what he was agreeing to.

He shook his head again. "I'm a submissive, Justin, not a slave."

Justin stroked his cheek. "A submissive who could enjoy giving control to a man he can trust to look after him far better than he ever looked after himself."

Luke looked down. He took Justin's hand away from his crotch and tried to focus again. "I play games, Justin. I don't live the whole lifestyle twenty-four hours a day, seven days a week. I don't want that."

"I'm not telling you how to run your life, sweetheart. I'm telling you that when you have sex with me, I will be in control, just as I have been from the start. The only difference will be that the rules I make about sex will apply when you are alone as well."

Luke hesitated. Taking Justin's hand away hadn't helped as much as he hoped. Justin was still there, still close inside his space. The subtle scent of his aftershave still hung in the air, tempting Luke to snuggle into his neck.

Justin kissed his lips again. "Try it and see what you think?" he suggested.

"And if I change my mind?"

"No problem. There wouldn't be any point in us doing something you don't enjoy, would there?"

No longer feeling like he was signing away control of his life forever, Luke nodded. If Justin wanted to try it then he would, at least then Justin would see he had made an effort. "So until I change my mind?"

"You need my permission to come."

Luke nodded his understanding. It wasn't so different from normal. There was no reason to be nervous. He could do this. Luke pulled himself together and tried to sound like he knew what he was doing. He tried to think of something to say. Luke was used to Justin controlling sex. This shouldn't be so difficult.

Justin took him by the hand and walked towards the main entrance. Luke followed blindly until Justin took a wrong turn. Justin smiled over his shoulder when Luke hesitated.

"I want to dance."

Luke nodded again. As they reached the floor, a rare slow song sung out over the speakers. Justin pulled Luke close. For a while they just swayed together. Justin slid one arm around Luke's waist to hold him close. His other hand rested on the back of Luke's head, encouraging him to rest his head on his shoulder. Luke didn't need much encouragement, he'd missed being close with his lover too much.

However, the idiot inside him hadn't been quite killed off by his earlier mistakes. "Are you sure you wouldn't prefer to dance with someone else?"

Justin pressed a kiss to the accessible temple. "Jealous?"

"No."

"I would be if I saw you dancing with another man," Justin whispered to him.

"Maybe a little bit jealous," Luke allowed after due consideration. "He was gorgeous."

"I wouldn't know, sweetheart. I spent the whole time looking at you."

It was temptingly close to the truth. Luke had looked away so many times, but every time he looked back Justin's gaze was still on him.

"You didn't have to dance with him if you didn't want to," Luke pushed.

"I wanted you to regret breaking up with me."

Luke tried to deny it.

Justin wouldn't hear him out. "I thought you broke up with me," he rephrased. "And I wanted you to miss me."

"I did," Luke whispered, tucking his face more firmly into Justin's shoulder.

They continued to sway. Luke pressed his body again Justin's. It was reassuring to feel the evidence Justin was as turned on as he was. His dominant still wanted him.

The song faded out to be replaced by a slowly building rhythm. Justin began to dance rather than sway. He turned Luke in his arms so his back rested against Justin's chest.

Resting a hand low on Luke's stomach, Justin guided him into the rhythm he wanted. Gradually, his hand stroked lower until he massaged Luke's erection. He pushed himself into Justin's hand. He was so desperate for contact, he forgot about everyone around them. He forgot about everything but Justin's hand in front of him and Justin's body behind him.

"You look amazing like this."

Luke tilted his head to the side, trying to focus in on what Justin said.

"Everyone's watching you — watching me touch you. Are you going to come for me, right here on the dance floor with everyone watching?" Justin whispered.

"Justin?"

"Yes, sweetheart."

Luke decided a bit more of the truth wouldn't hurt if it sped things up. "I haven't come since you walked out of my room. You could sell tickets for all I care."

Justin chuckled and held him even closer. "Does that make you an exhibitionist or just extremely horny?"

"Both." Luke tried to turn around in Justin's arms. Justin wouldn't let him. Luke persisted and eventually Justin allowed him to do as he wished. "You want them to see we're together? You want everyone in this room to know how I submit to you? Give the command. I'll get down on my knees in the middle of the dancers and prove it to you and everyone else."

Justin seemed amused. "As much as I enjoy your mouth, do you really think you can manipulate me so easily?"

Luke blinked.

"You'd find that easy, wouldn't you, sweetheart? Showing off how talented your mouth is to all your friends would really turn you on. But the idea I could make you come when you don't choose to – that scares the hell out of you. I don't know why, but it does."

Luke stopped dancing. They both stood perfectly still in the middle of the swaying and grinding couples. Luke didn't know where the words came from. Without ever realising the thought was in his head, he found the words on his lips. "I'm not a detail."

"And I told you that you could veto the important things, but you have to leave the details down to me," Justin said softly. He smiled.

Luke looked away and frowned.

"Have I ever suggested that I don't care if you enjoy what we do together?" Justin asked.

Luke shook his head. This was stupid. He sounded like an idiot and he wasn't going to have a conversation that made him look stupid. "If it's what you want, if you want me to come on the dance floor, do it," Luke said.

"No."

Luke hesitated. If Justin really wanted that, he would go along with it. He knew he still had ground to make up with his lover and he wasn't going to make a fool of himself throwing a hissy fit over something he should find easy. "Why not?"

"Do I want everyone to see we are together? Yes. And do I want them to see you want me? Of course. But when I allow you to come, I will be the only one watching you."

Luke stayed perfectly still. Doing whatever you wanted was dominant. Not doing what you want for any reason was inherently submissive. Caring what other people saw sounded like an excuse not to do what he knew Luke didn't want.

But Justin didn't sound submissive. He sounded calmly certain about what he wanted. Something still felt wrong.

"I'm possessive, but I'm not an exhibitionist, sweetheart. I won't share even the sight of you coming with anyone else. A real dominant knows when someone belongs to him. I don't have to prove the point."

Unable to think of anything to say, scared to part his lips in case unexpected words fell from them, Luke just nodded. The tiny movement restarted the world.

Justin led him back into the dance. He didn't make him come on the dance floor, but it was a close call at points. Justin took him right to the edge and made him hover there for what felt like hours. Each song wound into the next. Luke stopped listening to anything but the beat of his own heart, stopped registering anything but the rhythm of Justin's hips.

Even though he was achingly hard and frustrated, by the time they left, Luke felt more level in himself. He was back on track. Nothing changed. It was sex. It was sex with dating. It was sex with Justin dominant. But when it came down to the bone it was still just sex. Luke knew what he was doing when it came to sex. There was nothing to worry about.

Sitting in the passenger seat as Justin drove them back to his apartment, Luke turned his head against the rest to watch the other man.

"You wanted me to tell you about the creepy security guard," Luke remembered.

That caught Justin's full attention.

"He's not stalking me," Luke reported. "He had a bet on if we were screwing each other. He was watching me to win the bet. I told him we're screwing and we're monogamous. I think he wants us to make out in front of Tommy from the night shift to get his money."

Justin's lips twitched. "We'll see how it goes."

Luke could tell Justin was pleased with him for telling him. Some part of the tension drained from the car. The silence felt comfortable around them, and didn't change when they went up the stairs.

Luke couldn't help but remember the last time Justin was there. He'd been so slow and almost reverential with him. In hindsight, it was obvious Justin did everything he could think of to make sure Luke enjoyed himself. He really made it all about Luke during those weeks when Luke held back.

"What are you thinking?" Justin asked.

"You really thought I'd lost interest in you?" Luke countered, closing the front door behind them.

Justin shrugged. "It felt like you had trouble tipping over the edge."

Luke dropped the game, he dropped the submission. He leaned up against Justin and pulled him down for a slow, deep kiss filled only with honest desire. Justin allowed it and then smiled against Luke's lips as he took back control.

Submission and a preference for bottoming aside, Luke knew he wasn't a small man. Few of his lovers had been substantially bigger or stronger than him. That was his excuse for the yelp he let out when Justin picked him up as if he wasn't six foot tall with a fair layer of muscle over every inch of that height.

Justin laughed. He carried him through to the bedroom and tumbled onto the bed with him.

"And now I have you back, what should I do with you?" Justin leaned up on an elbow. He beamed down at Luke, appearing very happy with the state of his world.

"Out of ideas?" Luke asked. He had a few of his own if that was really true. He could be very inventive when he put his mind to it.

"I still have a few ideas," Justin reassured him. Trailing his finger tips up and down the front of Luke's black t-shirt, he burrowed under the material to stroke his bare skin. "And almost all of them involve you naked."

"Sounds good so far."

When Justin made no move to do so, Luke pulled his clothes off and dropped them off the side of the bed.

Justin made no effort to hide his admiration of the view. He studied Luke for a long time before he reached out to stroke his erection. "From now on, I'm the only one who touches you."

Luke nodded. Monogamy, they'd covered that.

"Including you. You don't jack yourself off without my explicit permission."

Try it. Think about it. See if you enjoy it. You can change your mind. Justin's earlier promise turned the demand into an invitation to give up control. And he knew Justin enjoyed getting him off—Justin really did give a damn if Luke enjoyed what they did together. The invitation wasn't a trick to make it all about what Justin wanted. Justin wasn't like most of the men he'd dated before—no matter how hard it was to remember that, he had to try.

Luke half nodded and then hesitated. "No masturbating," he agreed.

Justin raised an eyebrow at the change of wording.

"I'll still need to aim when I take a leak."

"I think I'll allow that," Justin chuckled. His finger tips traced lines along him. With great deliberation, he announced, "I'm going to screw you now."

Luke nodded his agreement. "Yes."

"You're not going to come."

The chances of that actually happening were microscopic. Luke nodded anyway. If Justin wanted him to aim for hoops he would never be able to jump through then at least he could enjoy himself while he made the attempt.

Apparently done with teasing, Justin put Luke on his hands and knees. He spent just enough time preparing him to make sure he was ready, but he didn't seek out his prostate. He didn't provide any stimulation other than what couldn't be avoided.

When he entered Luke, although he pulled him back close against his body and thrust as deeply into him as any man could get, the perfect angle wasn't achieved.

Luke tried to subtly shift his position.

Justin put his hands on Luke's hips and stopped him.

"Do you really think I made you come by accident, Luke?"

"What?"

Justin pulled him back so Luke sat astride Justin's knees while Justin knelt on the bed.

"Do you believe I found your prostate by luck? I know what you like, Luke. I know how to push you to the edge, and over the last few weeks you've given me a master class in what it takes to get you off."

He thrust up into Luke and rocked them together.

"But you haven't just taught me what you like, sweetheart. You've taught me dozens of different things I know you'll enjoy, but which I know you won't quite be able to get off on.

"You won't come without my permission, because you'll do as you're told. But at the same time, you won't come, because I won't give you the chance, Luke."

"You…" Luke tried to turn to face him while still impaled on Justin's erection. He couldn't twist far enough. And he couldn't think of a polite enough word to call someone who might take offence and not let him come at all. Uncertainty whirled inside him. He shrugged it off. Justin had earned a bit of trust.

Justin merely thrust up into him again. Luke gasped. It felt amazing. Every nerve ending tingled. But Justin was right. He wouldn't come from this. He would just become more and more frustrated.

And while Luke was held back, Justin wasn't trying to outlast anyone. He was free to enjoy himself at whatever pace he wanted. Luke rode him through his orgasm. He'd come second twice in a row. He'd proved his point. Luke was entirely comfortable with the idea Justin could outlast him at every single future encounter.

His problem was solved, a potential disaster was averted, sex was once more universally great.

Justin collapsed onto the bed next to him. Luke's hand crept to his cock.

"I told you not to touch, Luke."

Damn.

Luke dropped his hand back to his side. Looking over at Justin, the man's eyes were still shut. How the hell did he do that?

"I thought, since we understand each other now..." Luke began.

Justin smiled but didn't bother to open his eyes.

"I don't think you can count it as trying it to see if you like it, unless you give it a fair chance. Breaking the rules because you're a little bit frustrated is —"

"A little bit!" Luke yelled.

Justin chuckled.

"Nine days!" Luke reminded him. "When was the last time you came?"

"About two minutes ago."

"Before that," Luke protested.

"A few hours ago."

"You just screwed me without giving me the remotest chance of coming, you barely tuck your cock away between orgasms and you still have the nerve to call me *a little bit frustrated.*"

He threw his pillow at his lover and flopped back on the bed.

Justin caught the pillow and tossed it back with a deep rich laugh.

Luke held it over his face, the same way he had a week before. It smelt of Justin's aftershave again. It smelt wonderful. Luke took a deep breath and savoured the scent. Justin was back. His dominant was back. If he could just come then all would truly be right with the world.

"Hey," Justin pulled the pillow away from his face.

Luke took in his cheerful expression and sighed. This was Justin's show. Luke would come when he was given permission.

"You wouldn't prefer my hand, my mouth?" Justin tossed his earlier words back at Luke with a grin.

If he'd still had the pillow, Luke would have tried his aim a second time. "I want you," he said. "In whatever form you prefer." It wasn't easy to give the impression of bowing while lying on his back. Luke managed it with a slow nod and a speaking look.

Justin laughed and lethargically made his way down the bed.

Dominants who didn't think an ability to give incredible head was submissive, were right up there on Luke's list of the wonders of the world. He hadn't had the practice Luke had, but he was a quick learner. Justin knew what he was doing down there.

He was also resilient once he decided on the mood. Yes, Justin had proved he knew how to control Luke's libido better than Luke did himself during anal. As he began to tease with his lips and tongue, Luke knew he was in for the second act of the play—how to wrap your mouth around someone in amazing ways without letting them come.

"Since I'm going to have my mouth full for a very long time," Justin said, breaking contact for a few moments, "and since it is very rude to talk with your mouth full. Just this once, you don't need to wait for verbal permission to come."

Luke sent a silent prayer in thanks giving up to anyone who was listening.

"You just have to wait until I do something that offers you that opportunity."

"You..." *Polite*, Luke reminded himself.

The humour in Justin's eyes made Luke sure he would take any insult he could throw with as much fun as he'd caught the pillow, but Luke wasn't going to take any chances.

Justin was giving him an excellent blow job. That was a good thing. But as Justin managed to avoid any stimulation that could provide satisfaction, Luke found it hard to remember that anything so frustrating could be a good anything.

Justin's tongue slid over him again and again, swirling around the head and stroking against the pulsing veins. Murmuring his enjoyment just to let Luke taste the vibrations, Justin made no attempt to hide how much the dominant in him got off on the exertion of control or how much the man behind the dominant thrived on giving him pleasure.

Luke almost reconsidered his earlier assessment and decided there was a hell of a lot of sadist mixed into Justin's personality when, with one last glance at him,

Justin deep throated him and brought him to his climax just as easily as he'd corralled him at the edge for so long.

Good manners aside, Luke couldn't stop himself bucking into Justin's mouth. Justin rode out the movements without any trouble until Luke lay still again. Finally finding the energy to open his eyes, Luke looked across at Justin, now laying calm and content on the bed next to him.

"You look very smug," he accused.

Justin considered the accusation. "Yes," he allowed eventually, "I feel very smug indeed." He held out an arm and Luke quickly wriggled across the bed to lie in his embrace. He'd thought about this bit of the night more than he would ever admit out loud, he wasn't going to waste the moment by pouting.

With a half sigh, Luke had to admit he was exactly where he wanted to be, and he felt a little bit smug himself. Leaving Justin's arms for a brief moment, he pulled the blanket up over their cooling skin. Wrapping it snugly around their bodies, he cocooned them both in the soft white fabric.

"Do you need to go back to your place tonight?" Luke asked, casually. He would have a hell of a lot of trouble getting out the tangle of blankets if he wanted to leave in as big a rush as last time.

Justin idly stroked Luke's hair. "I can stay."

Luke nodded. The question was invitation enough. The actual words didn't need to be said... but something else did need to be said — or at least hinted at.

"Did you know there's a new Italian restaurant on Hamilton Street?"

Without looking up from his comfortable resting place, Luke knew Justin smiled above him. The hand continued to stroke his hair through a few moments of happy silence.

"Strange you should mention that," Justin said.

"It is?"

"We're going there tomorrow," he announced.

"We are?" Luke asked.

"Yes."

Evidently dinner was classified as a detail. Those were Justin's concerns.

Luke nodded and snuggled closer into his lover's embrace. "That sounds very, very perfect."

TIME TO DO

Dedication

To best friends and lovers, and especially to those who are lucky enough to find one person who can be both things to them at the same time.

Chapter One

Brennan Talbot was not going to stare at his best friend's arse. There was a line a gay man didn't cross while sharing a room with his straight best friend. He was going to stay on the right side of that line even if it killed him.

Turning around, Brennan held back a sigh. If he could just keep Rigby from bending over all the time, his life would be a hell of a lot easier. His friend possessed a truly wonderful backside, not to mention a preference for very tight jeans.

Brennan picked up yet another of Rigby's text books off the floor and placed it on his desk. "Where do you get all this stuff from anyway?" he asked.

Brennan risked a glance over his shoulder. At least his friend was standing up straight now.

Rigby shrugged. His shoulder muscles rippled under his t-shirt. He added another book to the growing pile on his desk. "It all just turns up somehow. Anyway, quit complaining. You're the one who insisted we rediscover the floor today."

Brennan looked around their room. Small patches of carpet were slowly starting to emerge between the layers of Rigby's junk. "I go home for one weekend and a bomb explodes," he muttered to himself. He doubted that Rigby was actually listening anyway. "You could at least have kept the debris on your side of the room."

Rigby chuckled at the familiar complaint. The low deep sound filled the small room and made Brennan smile in spite of his annoyance.

"I was looking for my locker keys," Rigby offered by way of explanation. "All the other stuff was in the way."

"So you threw it on the floor?" Brennan asked, putting a folder of history notes on the desk.

"Well, I usually ask you where stuff is and you tell me. You weren't here so I had to improvise. Are you studying *The Fall of the Roman Empire*?"

Brennan glanced at the book in Rigby's hand. "Doesn't really fit in with a Physics degree, does it?"

"Then I guess this one's mine, too." Rigby frowned at it and put it on the shelf above his desk. "I don't suppose you want to take a break and get something to eat?"

Brennan looked at the containers of food his mother sent back to the university with him. It was tempting, but he knew if they stopped before the floor was clear, the room would remain in the same state until the end of term.

"No," he said firmly. "Floor first, then food. I'll even share the cake my Mum made if we finish it in the next hour."

"That's blackmail," Rigby complained.

"I think you'll find it's bribery," Brennan corrected absentmindedly. He picked another folder up off the floor and read the title scrawled across it in Rigby's handwriting—*stuff*. Well, that was informative.

Brennan tossed it towards Rigby's desk. As it landed, the edge of the cardboard folder collapsed. Papers snowed down to the floor. Kneeling on a rare patch of carpet to pick them up, Brennan skimmed over a few lines on the top page.

It wasn't really snooping when the papers were spread out all over the carpet for anyone to read. Anyway, he'd known Rigby since they started nursery school. They didn't have any secrets from each other. Or to be entirely accurate, Brennan corrected himself, Rigby didn't have any secrets from him.

A glance identified it as some sort of to do list. Such a rare sign of organisation in Rigby's life had to be worth investigating further. Brennan read point number one—*get drunk*, and grinned. That was more like the Rigby he knew. There was a decisive tick by that point.

When Brennan read point number two—*go skinny dipping*— there was no chance he'd stop reading. An image of Rigby bare arse naked flashed across his mind and dropped straight to his crotch. That particular image had been carefully constructed over several months of sideways glances, but it was far from up to date.

Brennan might know he'd never get more than friendship from Rigby, but he wasn't prepared to lose that friendship by sneaking a peek at Rigby's cock in the showers after rugby practise. Not when the possibility of passing off his actions as teenage curiosity, or an innocently heterosexual interest in making comparisons, died the day he told Rigby he was gay.

There wasn't a tick next to skinny dipping. He wondered if it would it be considered morally wrong to convince a straight guy to go skinny dipping with him just so he could check him out. While he tried to work that out, Brennan's eyes trailed down to the next item on Rigby's to do list.

Have sex with a girl. Like he needed any extra proof Rigby was as straight as they come. It was very definitely ticked off. Rigby had happily worked his way through the female half of the university population since they'd arrived on campus. Brennan gave another mental sigh. Sometimes it took a hell of a lot of effort for him to pretend he was pleased for his friend about that.

He skipped through all the other ticked off points under the heading — each one representing one of the many and varied things Rigby wanted to do, and without exception had done, with girls.

Brennan went straight to point number four.

Have sex with a guy.

He blinked at the piece of paper. He read it again. He read it a third time, running his fingertip under the line of words, making sure there wasn't any other explanation. Rigby's spelling and his handwriting were terrible, but there weren't any long words in the sentence for him to get wrong.

Guy.

Sex.

All the important points were certainly there.

Brennan blinked again and stared down the list. There were subsections there too. Kiss. Touch. Oral. Anal. Everything Brendan had fantasised about doing with Rigby since before he could even remember.

Damn, Rigby really could do organised when he wanted to!

"You listening?" Rigby nudged Brennan's shoulder.

Brennan, still half kneeling by the broken folder, spun around. His balance deserted him. He collapsed in a messy heap of limbs at Rigby's feet. His head cracked against the wooden bed frame of Rigby's bed.

"Hey, you okay?" Rigby grabbed Brennan's arm and easily pulled the slightly smaller man to his feet.

Brendan clutched the list tight in his fist. He nodded automatically.

Step back. That was what he was supposed to do. He knew better than to linger in a straight guy's personal space too long.

"You hit your head or something?" Rigby asked with a frown. He put his hand on Brennan's head, stroking his fingers through the fine blond hair, looking for bumps.

Rigby was right there. And he'd written a list talking about kissing guys. And there wasn't a tick next to it. And he wasn't quite as straight as Brennan always thought. And his lips were right there.

He was a few inches taller than Brennan. Rigby needed to duck his head a little, before he could look straight into Brennan's eyes. "Do you know what the symptoms for concussion are?"

Brennan looked back at Rigby, the way he'd wanted to look at his best friend. He leaned forward. An inch was all it took.

Their lips met. Brennan's eyes dropped closed. Rigby gasped against his mouth. Brennan brushed their lips together again. Rigby began to pull back, trying to straighten up.

Gripping his shoulder, Brennan kept him where he was. He dropped the list and slid his other hand into Rigby's hair, tangling his fingers in the thick dark waves and pulling him back down to a comfortably kissable height.

Rigby tried to say something. All Brennan understood was the movement of Rigby's lips against his and that an open mouth was an invitation. He slid his tongue past Rigby's lips and moaned softly at the first touch of tongue against tongue.

Brennan leaned into the kiss, pressing his body against Rigby's and feeling each line of hard muscle through his clothes. Rigby's hands closed over his. He stepped away. He wouldn't let Brennan follow him. Brennan opened his eyes.

He met Rigby's gaze. He saw his expression. Shock. There was concern mixed in with it, but it was mostly shock.

Then Rigby half smiled. "You must have hit your head harder than I guessed." He let go of Brennan's hands.

Brennan stepped back. He'd kissed Rigby. Brennan shook his head. No, that couldn't be right. He couldn't have kissed Rigby, because Rigby was straight.

Straight men really wouldn't like gay guys kissing them, even if they were best friends. Brennan knew that. He knew he couldn't kiss Rigby.

He took another shaky step back. This wasn't happening.

"Bren, are you going to hyperventilate? Damn! Do you know if we've got a paper bag somewhere?" Rigby started looking around the room as if one might materialise at any moment.

"I hyperventilated once, Rig, when I was seven, that's thirteen years ago. You can stop going on about it now." Brennan took a deep breath. He risked a glance at his best friend.

Rigby hadn't taken a swing at him. He tentatively took that to be a good sign.

"You okay?" Rigby asked.

Brennan nodded. He pushed a hand through his hair. Another step back and he felt the edge of his desk behind him. Leaning against it, he tried to work out what to say. He started with the obvious. "I am *so* sorry."

Rigby shrugged and took a perch on the small patch of his own desk not covered in books and junk. "Don't worry about it."

Brennan licked his lips. He crossed his arms, barely resisting the urge to touch his mouth and trace the lines where his lips touched Rigby's. No other suitable words came to Brennan's mind. Silence descended.

"Shouldn't I be the one who's really freaked out?" Rigby asked after a while. "I'm the one who never kissed a guy before. You're supposed to be used to all this. It was just a kiss. Right? It's no big deal."

Kissing his best friend was a big deal. Kissing the guy he'd been in love with for the last three years was a huge deal. Anything involving Rigby was always an enormous deal in Brennan's world.

He forced a smile. The important thing was to keep what he could. He didn't want to lose Rigby's friendship on top of everything else. "You're not freaked out?" he checked.

Rigby shrugged. "Not really." He seemed to think about it for a while. "I kissed a guy," he seemed to muse on the topic for a moment. Then he nodded. That was it.

Brennan smiled and shook his head. He shouldn't have worried. He knew Rigby well enough to know nothing ever freaked him out. He'd displayed much the same reaction when Brennan had finally built up the courage to confess he was gay. Nod. Shrug. That's nice. Do you want to go for pizza now?

Everything would be fine and he even had the memory of a kiss as a bonus. Brennan nodded to himself. The situation simply called for light, friendly, banter — they were good at that. Brennan could do that.

"You can tick it off your list," he said.

"What list?"

Brennan's smile froze.

Rigby frowned. "Bren?"

"Your to do list," Brennan hinted.

Rigby's expression didn't change. He didn't even remember making the damn thing. Well, wasn't that just bloody perfect!

Lie. It was the obvious solution. He should lie. Except Rigby always knew when he was lying.

"Bren?"

With a sigh, Brennan looked around the floor and found the crumpled bit of paper. He handed it over and retreated to his nice neat desk on his side of the room.

Rigby read it. Brennan watched his eyes flitter across each line of messy handwriting.

"Do you have a pen?"

"A pen?" Brennan repeated blankly.

"So I can tick it off."

Brennan couldn't bite back a laugh filled with pure relief. He tossed a pen across to his friend.

Rigby took the top off. "I kissed a guy."

"Technically, you didn't."

"What?"

Brennan bit back a flinch and tried to work out when he lost any and all control of his mouth. For better or worse, Brennan realised he no longer had any choice but to keep going. "Technically you didn't kiss a guy," he explained, "a guy kissed you."

"Same thing."

Brennan shook his head. "Not even close."

"I might not have your experience with guys, but I have kissed, and been kissed, by a few girls in my time. It is the same thing," Rigby said with complete certainty.

Brennan shrugged. "Maybe it's different with a girl. But with two men, there's definitely a difference."

Rigby frowned down at the piece of paper. "I already ticked it off the list."

"So turn it into a cross," Brennan suggested.

Rigby nodded, but he didn't put pen to paper again. "It's different how?"

Brennan dropped his gaze to his hands. It wasn't exactly the first time they'd talked about his sex life. Rigby was scrupulous in treating him the same way he'd treat a straight friend—right down to casual enquiries over if he got lucky when he drove the thirty-seven miles to a gay bar in the neighbouring city.

"It just feels different," Brennan said lamely.

Moving away from the desk, he began picking things up again.

"Doesn't really answer the question," Rigby observed.

Without turning back to look at his friend, Brennan frowned and thought about his answer. He weighed each word very carefully before he spoke. "It's about control. Maybe that's why it's different with a girl. You're the guy, she's the girl. Nothing's going to change that." He picked up another book. "With two guys, anything could happen. You can tell a lot from the way a guy kisses you. It makes you feel different too."

Rigby didn't laugh. He didn't make a joke. He didn't interrupt.

"If I kiss a guy, I feel like I'm in control," Brennan went on. "I know what I'm doing, I know what I want and I'm pretty sure things are going to go as I say unless I lose control of the kiss. I don't know about other guys, but when a man kisses me, and he makes damn sure he keeps control of the kiss, it's nothing like the same. He's in charge. I'm just along for the ride."

"So the first kiss decides who...?" Rigby trailed off as he ran out of appropriate vocabulary.

"Decides who tops and who bottoms?" Brennan filled in for him. He smiled and shook his head. "It's not as simple as that."

"What do you prefer?"

Brennan hesitated as he picked up another book. That was a whole new level of interest in his sex life. "Depends on what mood I'm in. Depends on the guy I'm with."

With Rigby there would be no depends. While he was as flexible as he claimed, Brennan wouldn't deny having far more day dreams about Rigby catching for him rather than pitching to him.

"So you like being kissed?"

Heat flooded to Brennan's face. Rigby was still talking about kissing. He sent up silent thanks that chance had worded his answer not to be too specific. As for kissing... Brennan didn't even have to think about his answer. He wanted to be kissed. He wanted to know Rigby was in control — to know Rigby wanted him as much as he had always wanted Rigby.

"Yeah, I like being kissed," he admitted, not that there was any chance of it now.

Rigby stood up. He put his hand on Brennan's shoulder.

Brennan turned around.

"I'm not changing teams," Rigby said.

Brennan tried to turn away. "I never said you should."

Rigby held him in place. "I'm not finished."

Brennan looked up at his friend and waited for his verdict.

"I'm not changing teams," Rigby repeated. "But, since I've already ticked the point off my list, maybe I should do it properly."

"You want to kiss me?" Brennan said, amazed with how calm he sounded.

"Do you mind?"

Brennan pulled himself together enough to shake his head.

No hesitation. Rigby's lips moulded against his. His tongue slid, slick and confident, into Brennan's mouth.

Brennan bit back a whimper. His lips parted, encouraging his friend to deepen the kiss. Brennan risked slipping his tongue into Rigby's mouth in return. Rigby didn't object, but he made damn sure he stayed in control of the kiss at every turn. The hand gently cupping Brennan's face slid into his hair, tilting his head back at just the angle Rigby wanted.

Brennan stopped thinking. He stopped breathing. He gave up doing anything but enjoying the kiss while it lasted.

Shit. This shouldn't be happening. Every sensible part of his psyche screamed at Rigby Matthews, telling him to pull away. He was kissing a guy. He was kissing Brennan.

Rigby licked his way back into his best friend's mouth as thoughts flashed one after another into his mind. Brennan's hair was too short—it didn't give Rigby enough to hold onto. But at six foot, he was taller than any girl he'd ever kissed and not getting a crick in his neck felt good. His lips were firmer than a girl's and there was no chance he'd freak out because

94

Rigby smudged his lipstick. Worryingly enough, he also realised his best friend was an astonishingly good kisser.

And, above all that, one thought ran screaming around Rigby's brain. This truly was a bloody stupid way to prove he wasn't freaked out by Brennan's kiss.

Still, stupid or not, he couldn't just let Brennan panic. He'd looked so terrified when he stepped back after the kiss, so sure Rigby was going to throw a punch. After years spent coming to Brennan's rescue, he couldn't stop himself from trying to fix everything when he saw that particular expression on his best friend's face.

It was just a kiss—no different to warning bullies away when they were twelve years old and Brennan hadn't had the punch to back up his sarcasm. No different than taking the flack for some silly practical joke—because he knew his Dad would laugh, but Brennan's would ground him for a month.

It was just a kiss. It was just a straight guy kissing his male best friend. There was nothing strange about that. It couldn't be too strange, Rigby reassured himself, because right there, right then, the kiss felt sort of right.

Brennan touched his cheek, trailing his fingers along the dark shadow Rigby hadn't bothered to shave away. Rigby copied the action. Brennan was so fair it was hard to tell if he'd shaved just by looking at him, but now Rigby knew he had. He ran his thumb across Brennan's jaw again. There wasn't even a trace of stubble, just an unfamiliarly square jaw line.

Homophobic guys were the ones who weren't comfortable in their own sexuality. Rigby never doubted that. He knew he was entirely comfortable with Brennan being gay because he was completely comfortable being straight.

Brennan gasped into the kiss and lapped at his lips, pleading once more for admittance. For the first time, Rigby realised he was so comfortable with the absolute knowledge he was straight, he could actually get a hard on kissing his best friend. Rigby adjusted the angle of his body so Brennan wouldn't notice.

Kissing had to stop at some point. It needed to stop or progress into something more than a kiss. Rigby knew he shouldn't have to think about the decision. He slowly pulled back a few inches. Brennan's eyes stayed closed, his lips remained parted. Rigby only just resisted the temptation to dive back in for another brief touch of lips.

Brennan stepped back before he opened his eyes. He turned away before he looked up from the carpet.

Rigby stepped back as well. He pressed the heel of his hand to his erection, wishing it away before Brennan noticed its presence. Luckily Brennan didn't seem to be in a rush to look at him. Rigby caught sight of his profile. He saw the blush on his best friend's cheeks.

Rigby cleared his throat. "I guess I can cross it off the list for real then."

Brennan nodded.

Rigby looked through the piles on his desk and tried to remember where he put the pen. Brennan slid another biro under his hand and retreated back over to the other side of the room. Rigby ticked the kiss very firmly off the list.

An hour later, everything in the room was back in its rightful place. Brennan didn't tease him about the mess. Rigby didn't have the heart to moan about the tidying up. Neither of them seemed to know quite how to break the silence.

Rigby studied the back of Brennan's head. He'd just give his friend a bit of space. By tomorrow everything would be back to normal.

* * * *

Three days later normal was a distant memory.

Rigby stared at the back of Brennan's head again, this time across the shadowy room in the middle of the night. Brennan always slept curled up into a little ball with his back to the room — ever since he was little and they slept over at each others' houses and had camping trips in each others' back gardens.

Rigby turned on his side and looked at the small shape under the blanket on the opposite bed. Brennan might not sport quite as much muscle as his friend, but he was hardly a small man. It was hard to believe anyone of his height and build could fold himself up into such a tiny shape.

Three days without sarcastic put downs and moaning about the state of their room was wearing on Rigby's nerves. The kiss had shocked the hell out of him, and Rigby could only imagine how it felt to someone who liked guys, but this was getting stupid.

It was just a kiss. Rigby flopped over onto his back and stared at the ceiling. He brushed his finger tips over his lips. His other hand clenched into a fist as he remembered how hard it was to gain a purchase on

Brennan's short blond hair. He blinked at the image of big blue eyes looking up at him when he pulled away.

Rigby pushed the memory away as quickly as he could. The important thing was to get back to normal. He frowned at the ceiling. It was that bloody list. They'd ticked one sodding item off, and it screwed everything up. Rigby slid his hand down into the space between the mattress and the wall and retrieved the list from its hiding place. In the faint light spilling into the room from the gap in the curtains, he could just make out the lettering.

He didn't even know why he put all that stuff about guys on there, except he'd made it just after Brennan came out to him and at the time he had wondered if... Rigby sighed. Teenage curiosity could be a real bitch when it came back to bite you on the arse.

That's all it had been though, he reminded himself. Teenage curiosity. If Brennan had found religion when they were that age, Rigby was sure he'd have thought about praying on occasions too. As it was, Brennan found men and Rigby had thought about...

He turned over, trying to find a comfortable position on the thin mattress. Rigby liked girls. He'd always enjoyed having sex with girls. That had to look like pretty conclusive proof of heterosexuality in anyone's eyes. Rigby was straight. He would always be straight. He nodded to himself.

Still, no matter how straight he was, waiting for normality to click into place wasn't working. Rigby would just have fix it himself. Even if it meant finishing the list. Rigby hesitated, tapping the thin sheet of paper against his knuckles.

Finishing the list would certainly get Brennan back on the level. He never seemed to think twice about a guy once he screwed him, as far as Rigby could work out, Brennan had never had a relationship with a man that lasted more than a night. Whatever sexual spark Brennan had with someone seemed to die once the flame was fully explored.

Rigby read the list over in the half light. He could do that. He could have one go of everything—just to get it out of Brennan's system. Then they could go back to how things should be. Brennan would never have to worry about some latent spark of homophobia in the back of his friend's mind, and Rigby could get back to being straight and very happy about being that way.

He nodded to himself again. He could do that—for Brennan.

* * * *

"We should finish the list." Rigby watched his friend carefully, trying to gauge his reaction.

Brennan's hands froze above the keyboard but he didn't take his eyes off his lap top. His fingers started moving over the keys again, flying as fast as ever. "What list?"

Rigby dropped the list on the keyboard. He looked over Brennan's shoulder and read the last half a dozen lines of type on the screen—complete gibberish. Rigby grinned. "My list," he specified.

Brennan stopped trying to type. "You want to go skinny dipping?"

Rigby spun Brennan's computer chair around and forced his friend to face him properly. Surprised blue eyes flashed up to him and then looked quickly down.

"We'll have one go through the whole list. We'll both get it out of our system. Then we'll get back to normal."

"We're already back to normal," Brennan protested. He tried to turn away.

Rigby put his hands on either side of the chair back and kept Brennan where he was. "No, we're not. If we were back to normal you'd have laughed at what I just said and thrown out some sarcastic comment about how straight guys have never been your type."

Brennan said nothing.

"I started something last Sunday," Rigby told him. "We have to finish it."

Brennan shook his head. "This is a really screwed up idea."

"You say that every time I get an idea."

"And I'm always right—every idea you've ever had ended with us getting in trouble," Brennan reminded him.

"But you always go along with them anyway, so just quit stalling and skip straight to the part where you grudgingly decide to do as I say—it will save us both a lot of time."

Brennan took a deep breath. "Rig—you're straight. I don't know if someone forgot to explain the concept to you, but straight guys don't have sex with other guys. It's part of the bloody definition."

Rigby checked his watch. He sat on his bed, leaned back against the wall and settled to wait. "Let me know when you get to the bit where you agree with me, okay."

"You haven't thought this through," Brennan complained.

Rigby wasn't particularly worried by the statement. Brennan always said something similar at this point in the debate.

"You get some stupid notion into your head and go off all half cocked," Brennan went on.

Rigby grinned. "I assumed whole cocks would be involved, but hey, you're the expert…"

"You're insane." Brennan stood up and started to walk around the room. It was a small room. Four paces either way and he needed to turn around.

"You're going to get dizzy if you keep walking around in circles," Rigby warned.

Brennan finally stood still. He took another deep breath. "Why are you doing this? What's the punch line?"

"Have I ever joked about something like this with you?"

Brennan looked down. They both knew the answer. They teased each other about everything else, but Brennan's preference for men was not fair game. "No," Brennan admitted softly. "You haven't."

"Then I guess the ball's in your court. I've got a lecture now." Rigby handed Brennan the list as he grabbed his bag and headed for the door. "Let me know what you decide when I get back."

An early morning lecture was never the highlight of Rigby's week, but even hangovers and insomnia never caused so few notes to be taken or so few thoughts to lodge in his head.

Rigby tapped his pen against his knee. If his friend said he wasn't up for it then he'd just have to think of another way to get Brennan back to normal. That's what this was all about after all. His own thoughts about having sex with Brennan weren't the point.

No, Rigby watched the pen bounce off his knee, his thoughts weren't the point at all. Nothing changed for *him* the moment he kissed Brennan.

Chapter Two

When he saw Brennan sitting on his bed, wedged into the corner with both their pillows behind his back, Rigby knew his friend hadn't quite reached the reluctantly agreeable stage.

"I still think it's a stupid idea," Brennan announced, keeping his eyes on his reading book.

Rigby dropped his bag on his bed and grabbed a can of coke from the little fridge in the corner of the room. He tossed a second one across to Brennan.

Catching it one handed, Brennan considered the can carefully.

Rigby sat on his desk and waited.

"Are you going through some sort of bi-curious phase or something?" Brennan demanded.

Rigby shook his head. "I'm still straight."

Brennan nodded.

Rigby took a swig of the sweet, fizzy liquid and licked his lips. "Maybe it's the type of thing even a straight guy should try once before he dies," he offered. He'd come to that conclusion half-way through his lecture and he was rather pleased with it. Any inclination he felt towards gay sex was just a product of normal, healthy, heterosexual curiosity.

"No, it's not." Brennan sounded really certain. "Because by your logic, I should screw a girl before I die and the idea really doesn't appeal."

"You've never tried it?" Rigby asked.

"No."

"Never even been curious about what it's like with a girl?" Rigby pushed.

"No."

"Maybe you should give it a go. I really didn't realise how much fun kissing a guy could be until I tried it," Rigby pointed out. He would never have believed Brennan would give him the best kiss of his life before it actually happened.

Brennan hesitated. He closed his eyes for several long seconds. "Once through the list?" he asked as he finally opened his eyes again.

Rigby nodded.

"Then you go back to being properly straight?"

He nodded again.

"I'm an idiot," Brennan muttered.

Rigby grinned. "You always say that before you agree with me."

"At least I'm consistent," Brennan muttered. He set his book aside. "What point do you want to tick off first?" He picked the list up off his bed side table and tossed the crumpled piece of paper across the room.

Snagging the paper mid air, Rigby considered his options. Brennan was the planner. Rigby flew by the seat of his pants so often he should get air miles from

Levi's. He tossed the paper back across the room. "You pick. Alphabetical. Numerical. You're the expert on organisation."

Brennan smiled. "It's not expertise that's important here. You're forgetting, Rig, I've already done everything on the gay section your list. And I've gone skinny dipping too."

An image of Brennan stark naked with nothing but little droplets of water clinging to his skin, tracing intricate patterns down his body, launched itself into Rigby's mind. He quickly pushed it away. He was a straight guy helping out a friend. That was as far as this would go. Naked visuals were not a required part of the plan.

"We'll take them in order," he said, because he had to say something.

"I can't see how a hand job from a guy would be *that* different from a girl," Brennan said. "It would be better of course, but a hand job is still a hand job."

"How do you know it would be better if you've never done anything with a girl?" Rigby asked.

Brennan crossed the room and stood close to Rigby, way inside his personal space. "Do you really think any woman could have as much practise stroking a guy's cock as an actual guy?" he asked.

Rigby swallowed, he shrugged. It slowly started to dawn on him that he'd never encountered this side of Brennan's personality before.

"How many times have you jacked yourself off since you worked out what your cock was really for, Rig? You're straight and you could still probably give a guy a better hand job than any woman who's ever touched you."

Rigby couldn't even work out if that was a compliment or not. He tried to push away the memory of all the times he'd lain on the other side of the room to Brennan and waited until his friend was asleep before he took himself in hand then went to sleep himself.

Brennan put his hand on his knee. Rigby stared at it in fascination.

"Are you going to freak out if I touch you?"

"I don't freak out." Rigby was the calm one. He repeated the fact several times inside his mind. Brennan panicked, Rigby stayed calm. It was the way the world worked.

Brennan cupped him through his jeans. The heat from his hand soaked through the worn denim. Rigby froze. For several long seconds, Brennan's hand just rested there. Then he began moving his fingers in a slow deliberate motion, massaging him through his jeans.

Nothing occurring through a couple of layers of fabric should feel so good. Getting a hard on under Brennan's hand should feel embarrassing. Rigby caught his lip between his teeth and bit back a moan.

Brennan watched his hand with the same deliberate expression he used to wear doing lab work in science classes. He looked up. Rigby transferred his gaze to Brennan's hand.

"Do you want to take your jeans off, or would you prefer to come in your pants?"

Rigby snapped his gaze back up to Brennan's.

His friend smiled, not the smug sarcastic look Rigby somehow expected, a look saying this is my world, keep up or don't bother playing. No matter which side of his personality he was channelling to the foreground, Brennan was still Brennan. The smile offered Rigby an out. It said—if this isn't what you want keep your clothes on and we'll laugh this off.

It was so tempting to brush it all aside, pretend it was just a joke. Rigby knew what would happen if he did. Brennan would make some sarcastic comment about him sticking to girls because he couldn't keep up with a guy. Rigby would think of some suitable response, and that would be the end of it.

Rigby stood up. Brennan's hand immediately dropped away from him. He took a step back. Rigby undid the top button on his jeans. Brennan faltered in the middle of another step back. Another button gone, Brennan met Rigby's eyes.

There weren't many buttons left for Rigby to undo. He didn't have long to change his mind.

Buttons, in Brennan's opinion, were one of the many wonders of the world—especially when they were being undone.

He swallowed down his nerves. Rigby was actually doing this. This was actually happening. All he had to do was not panic and he might actually get to have sex with his best friend.

Rigby undid the last button on his jeans. Brennan tried to remember how to breathe. He was supposed to be the one who knew what he was doing. He couldn't let his friend think he was as clueless as he felt. Brennan's body, bored with waiting for his mind to catch up, stepped forward. He slid his hands inside Rigby's open fly, massaging his shaft through his boxers.

Every second was an extra blessing, something he never expected to get. As each moment passed, Brennan expected Rigby to push him away, but it didn't happen.

Brennan slid his hand past the thin cotton barrier and wrapped his hand around Rigby's cock. Skin met skin. Brennan stared down at his hand, fascinated by the sight of his pale skin against the darker skin of Rigby's shaft.

His friend thrust slightly then held still, tension running through his body. Brennan itched to touch, to run his hands all over Rigby's body. He longed to strip his friend's clothes away so he could see some of those muscles up close and, for once in his damn life, be allowed to stare for however long he wanted.

Brennan gave himself a mental shake. If he didn't ask for too much, he might be able to keep what Rigby was already offering. Brennan pushed Rigby's boxers just far enough out of the way, just so he had a bit of room to work. Rigby made no comment.

Old shower room peeks didn't do him justice — Brennan had seen enough to know Rigby was hung, but he'd underestimated his friend. Rigby's rapidly hardening cock was magnificent. Brennan slid his hand up the length and circled the head with his palm.

Rigby pushed against his hand.

Brennan smiled, not the least surprised. He'd always known Rigby would like everything fast and hard. He was that type of guy. Brennan tightened his grip a little, gauging Rigby's responses and working out what he would enjoy most as he became fully hard within Brennan's grip.

Rigby thrust into his hand again. Brennan tightened his grip a little further and slightly sped up his strokes. Rigby's hand wrapped over his fist. Demanding he take up a certain grip, he guided Brennan's hand into exactly the rhythm he wanted.

Control. Rigby liked to call the shots. For a few moments Brennan let himself pretend things were different. He let himself enjoy Rigby's control over the situation. But only for a few moments, then Brennan forced himself to remember the truth.

This was a student bedroom, not the type of leather bar Brennan liked to visit on the weekends. Rigby wasn't a dominant gay man taking control of his submissive. He was straight and vanilla, and he wasn't pushing Brennan towards submission, he was just making him irrelevant.

Brennan slid his hand out from under Rigby's grip. Rigby frowned and grabbed his wrist.

"I don't need you to teach me how to do this, Rig," Brennan told him seriously. "If you want to call all the shots, fine, but you don't need my hand in the way while you jack yourself off."

Rigby's grip on his wrist didn't ease. "Your way or no way?" he asked.

Brennan forced himself to meet Rigby's gaze and stand his ground. For a moment, he thought he saw something like possession, something like dominance in Rigby's eyes. He shook his head. Wishful thinking wasn't going to change the world.

"You can work your curiosity out on me, Rig," he said simply. "But don't treat me like I'm irrelevant. A man's hand comes with a man attached to it. If you want me to touch you, that's great, but let me touch you or there's really no point."

"Strange—I never pegged you as a control freak," Rigby grumbled.

"Strange—I've always pegged you as one," Brennan shot back.

He thought that it was all over when Rigby let go of his wrist. Then, before Brennan could step away, Rigby put his hands on the desk, one on either side of his hips. The look in his eye told Brennan that his friend was actually waiting, very impatiently, for him to get on with it. He wrapped his hand around Rigby's erection again. Velvety soft skin slid through his fingers. Swirling his palm over the head, he collected the trace of pre-cum leaking from the slit. There wasn't enough to slick Rigby's shaft properly.

Brennan let go for the briefest possible moment. He quickly licked his palm and let his saliva ease the friction as he took up his own rhythm rather than the one his friend demanded. Rigby looked less than impressed, but Brennan knew that the other guy doing something that you wouldn't do yourself was half the fun—it was practically the whole point of getting a hand job off someone else.

He'd felt enough hands on him to learn a few tricks he wouldn't have worked out during solo experimentation. The kind of things he'd guess most straight guys didn't have the right contacts to learn. Stopping at just the right moment, he took his hand away.

Rigby thrust into the empty air. He cursed under his breath. "I never pegged you as a tease either," he complained.

Brennan's lips twitched into a smile at the look on Rigby's face. "It's only a tease if you don't follow through in the end." As if there was any chance he would really stop while Rigby was willing to go on. He teased Rigby's foreskin between his fingers and followed the line of the vein along the underside of his cock.

A trace of taste from the pre-cum Brennan licked off his palm lingered on his tongue. Only the possibility of being allowed to explore the oral route another time and stretch out Rigby's gay experiment for as long as possible kept him off his knees. He softened his touch when he wrapped his fist back around Rigby's shaft.

For a few minutes it seemed possible to make the hand job last forever. But even if Rigby let him play at being in control, Brennan was under no real illusions. Rigby was humouring him for a while. It didn't matter if Brennan was the only one of them who liked leather. He still knew he would never be the dominant in their relationship—be it friendship or anything else.

"Bren?" in a specific tone of voice was all it took to make Brennan remember that. He retook the earlier firmer grip and settled into a rhythm designed to complete rather than prolong his friend's pleasure.

Rigby's head dropped back. Brennan looked from his cock to his face and back again and again, trying to look at both at just the right moment. Rigby came. Trails of his semen splattered over Brennan's hand as he kept pumping Rigby's cock through his orgasm.

His gaze settled on Rigby's face. He could see a cock come in his hand any night of the week. If this was the only time he'd ever see such pleasure in his friend's expression he had to make the most of it.

Brennan only looked away when Rigby blinked his eyes open. He grabbed a tissue from his desk and tossed another to his friend. Turning his back to give him a little bit of privacy to tidy himself up, Brennan listened to fabric rustle as Rigby straightened his clothes.

He just got Rigby off. Brennan grinned, safe out of Rigby's line of sight. He just got his straight best friend off. He shifted his stance a little. As cool as that was, it left Brennan with a problem. He forced a deep breath into his lungs, trying to calm himself down, but the air brought with it the scent of Rigby's arousal and did nothing to help his situation.

Rigby wanted to try out a guy. Brennan was under no confusion about what that meant. The only thing he'd get in return was some really great masturbation fodder for his collection of Rigby flavoured fantasies. Thinking about jacking off to the memory didn't help Brennan either.

He sighed to himself. If he ignored his erection for long enough it would go away — basic biological fact. Brennan forced air into his lungs again and again. It would be far from the first time he spoke to his friend while hiding an erection. It didn't have to be a problem.

"Are you still going down to the students' union later?" Brennan asked. His practise at not letting Rigby see how turned on he was held him in good stead — his voice didn't even waver.

"Aren't you getting ahead of yourself?"

Brennan tried to make his mind work through a dense fog of arousal. "You want to grab a pizza or something first?"

Rigby usually preferred to eat on the way back, unless he happened to hook up with some girl at the bar. Brennan was pretty sure food temporarily dropped to the bottom of Rigby's list of priorities on those nights.

"Pizza wasn't quite what I intended to grab," Rigby said. He turned Brennan around.

Brennan looked up at him. It took him a moment to catch on. He shook his head. "You don't have to do that."

Rigby just stood there, right inside Brennan's personal space, at a temptingly touchable distance, waiting for an explanation.

"You're straight, remember," Brennan said. He had to remember too. Straight. "I didn't start this up as tit for tat."

"You didn't start anything at all. I did. And don't flatter yourself that you could force me into doing anything I wasn't up for."

Brennan licked his lips. He swallowed and almost choked as his throat went dry. Yes, there was probably an ethical component to the question he should consider at this point. But hell, Rigby was offering him a hand job. No one could expect complex thought processes at this point. Brennan gave up and nodded on general principle.

That was apparently enough for Rigby.

He undid Brennan's fly. Hooking his fingers into his boxers, Rigby tugged them down along with his jeans. He obviously didn't think Brennan needed to be broken into the idea as carefully as Brennan had approached him. Rigby slid the material down, completely exposing Brennan, and wrapped his fist around his erection.

Brennan gasped. He came embarrassingly close to coming on the first touch. Rigby grinned down at him as if he knew, as if he liked knowing it.

There was no fuss, no working out what Brennan would like. Rigby gave what he wanted to give and Brennan took it without comment. He couldn't ignore the fact that, gay or straight, Rigby would be an awesome dominant if he ever ventured towards the leather end of the sexual spectrum.

Brennan bit his lip. *Make it last*, he told himself. If he came in the first minute he'd never be able to look Rigby in the eye again. If he came that soon he'd only have a minute's worth of memories to fall back on next time he was with some stranger in a bar and wasn't actually enjoying the experience enough to get off on it.

Rigby's rhythm changed and faltered.

Brennan looked up at him. He saw the frown between Rigby's dark eyebrows deepen.

Rigby stopped.

He took his hand away.

Closing his eyes, Brennan tried as hard as he could to push his disappointment aside. Straight, he repeated to himself. You can't blame a straight man for not wanting to get you off. At least he tried it out. At least he'd felt Rigby's hand on him for a few minutes. It was more than he'd ever hoped for before. It was stupid to feel cheated now.

Rigby took Brennan by the waist and turned him around. Brennan suddenly found Rigby pressed up close behind him, Rigby's fly pressed against his bare arse.

Brennan froze.

Rigby took him in hand again. "That's better," he murmured, once more stroking Brennan hard and fast. "The weird angle was messing up my rhythm."

He actually expected coherent conversation at his point? Brennan just about managed to nod. Rigby was only used to touching himself, he needed to use the same angle. That was okay. Oh, who was he kidding, Brennan knew damn well he'd stand on his head if it made Rigby keep doing what he was doing.

Looking down his body, he watched Rigby's hand move over his erection with perfect confidence. Brennan remembered the first time he'd made out with another guy. He'd been a nervous wreck. It was just like his friend to jump into it as if it was the most natural thing in the world.

Brennan tried not to push his arse back against Rigby's fly, but as Rigby dragged him closer and closer to the edge, it was almost impossible. Even on his own, Brennan liked to switch things up a little, make himself wait and work the final bit of pleasure. Rigby didn't mess around with any of that bull. He set his rhythm and he stuck to it. Simple, straight forward and completely amazing.

Brennan fought desperately to keep control of his body. He put his hand over Rigby's hand asking him to calm it down a little. Rigby's grip tightened. Brennan whimpered.

"Yes or no," Rigby whispered in his ear. "You can say stop. But slow down isn't an option. The hand comes with a man attached to it, right?"

Brennan bit back a moan but dropped his hand away. Rigby went back to exactly what he was doing. Damn if Brennan didn't know in that moment he'd use the exact same rhythm whenever he was on his own and thinking of his friend.

Rigby's other hand had rested on Brennan's waist, holding him still so he could jack him off as he pleased. Then it dropped down to massage Brennan's balls. Brennan rocked between Rigby's body and his hand as Rigby rolled the tightening sacs in his fingers. His touch was so practiced, so perfect, Brennan knew it was exactly how Rigby touched himself.

Brennan closed his eyes, groaning his pleasure when Rigby began to press his crotch against Brennan's arse, pushing him forward, pushing Brennan's cock more and more quickly into his hand.

For a moment Brennan felt as if he wasn't really there, Rigby was pretending to jack himself off just like he'd tried to pretend when they were the other way around. Brennan tensed. He tried to push the idea away. Even if it was true, he didn't want anything to screw up this memory. Was it really so bad to know exactly how Rigby liked to masturbate? Wasn't that good information for his fantasies about watching Rigby jack himself off?

It was no good, he still hated knowing Rigby was writing his presence out of the best moment in his life.

"Come on, Bren," Rigby whispered in his ear. "Come for me."

Those words changed everything. Brennan's fantasy came back into focus. He gave up any effort to hold back. Brennan came all over Rigby's hand, bucking between his fist and his fly again and again until he eventually fell still and silent. Rigby let go of his cock but when Brennan went to step away, he coaxed him to stay leaning back against him.

Rigby cleaned him up while he wiped off his own hand. He even fastened Brennan's jeans up, tucking his cock all snug back into place. And he still didn't nudge Brennan away.

"If I'd known ticking off the points would be so much fun, I'd have shown you the list ages ago," Rigby told him.

It was Brennan's cue to pull himself together. He nodded his agreement and retreated to his own side of the room. "What now?" he asked, leaning against his desk.

Rigby thought about it for a moment. "Pizza," he declared with certainty.

"Pizza?" Brennan echoed blankly.

"With extra everything," his friend specified.

Brennan blinked at him.

Rigby grinned. "I'm hungry. Pizza first and then the students' union."

He paused and considered his options for afterward. The usual choice was find a girl and get laid. Brennan forced a smile, ready to agree that was a great idea too.

"Movie Marathon," Rigby decided. "Come on—I'll even let you pick the movies if you hurry up."

Brennan tried to switch mental tracks. He failed.

Rigby grabbed his coat. "Come on. If you're not in the pizza place in time to order for yourself, I'm ordering for both of us and you lose the right to complain about what toppings I put on yours."

* * * *

Rigby tossed a kernel of popcorn in the air and caught it in his mouth.

Brennan pretended to watch the movie rather than Rigby.

"Want some?" Rigby offered him the popcorn tub.

Brennan took a handful. Salty, just like the taste he's snuck of Rigby earlier. Brennan smiled to himself. Hand jobs should make it more awkward between them, but in some bizarre way it levelled out the kiss. It made everything a friendly experiment—for Rigby at least.

As for himself, Brennan gave a mental shrug. He'd been in love with Rigby for so long he could just keep going as normal. The constant state of awareness, following every move Rigby made, always knowing if his friend was happy or sad, it all blended together after this length of time.

Brennan flinched. A piece of popcorn bounced off his head.

"I won't let you pick the film again if you're just going to day dream through it."

"I was just thinking," Brennan said.

"Careful it doesn't become a habit. You'll never graduate if you spend all your time in university thinking about stuff."

Brennan grabbed another handful of popcorn. He focused his eyes on the screen.

Rigby paused the DVD. "Okay. I give up, what are you thinking?"

Brennan shrugged. "Nothing special. Just thinking."

"Susan was right—you're weird."

"Your last girlfriend thought I was weird?" Brennan asked.

Rigby caught another piece of popcorn between his lips. "Actually, she thought I was weird. You were weird by association with me. But it sounds better if she just thought you were weird."

"Why are you weird?" Brennan asked.

Rigby shrugged.

"Weird as in weird or weird as in kinky?" Brennan asked. He stared intently at the frozen screen. That was okay wasn't it? Guys could talk about sex without it being weird just because one of them was gay, just because one of them was involved in a gay experiment.

"No, the complaint was definitely about the weird sort of weird. I think she would have liked the kinky sort of weird," Rigby said, slouching a little more comfortably in his seat.

Brennan nodded. "What about you?" he asked, as if it was just friendly curiosity prompting the question. As if he wasn't wondering if there was any chance he could get a bit of leather into Rigby's to do list.

"What about me?" Rigby asked.

"Do you prefer double choc chip with sprinkles and whipped cream, or are you strictly a vanilla man?" Brennan asked, trying desperately not show how much he wanted him to say the former.

"Vanilla," Rigby said firmly.

Brennan nodded. What a waste of a natural dominant...

"With maybe a little bit of chocolate sauce on the side," Rigby clarified.

Brennan nodded again, wondering just how much kink chocolate sauce represented.

"And maybe a touch of whipped cream," Rigby added.

Brennan glanced at Rigby out of the corner of his eye.

Rigby put the movie back on. He grinned at the screen. "And I guess a few sprinkles never hurt anyone."

Even though he knew Rigby was just teasing, possibilities raced through Brennan's head. He picked up a cushion, lying next to him on the sofa in the common room and placed it, as discreetly as possible, over his lap.

* * * *

"Do you have plans for this evening?" Brennan asked, trying his damnedest to sound casual, trying to sound as if he wasn't hoping to spend the evening ticking something else off Rigby's list.

"Alice Walker," Rigby said absentmindedly. "We could do something afterwards if you like."

Brennan quickly shook his head. "I already have plans," he lied.

Rigby nodded. To Brennan's intense relief Rigby seemed too distracted by his upcoming date to notice the lie or to ask him what those plans were.

A few minutes later Rigby was out of the door. Brennan stared at the closed door for a few minutes. Damn, he was stupid sometimes. It was a to do list. It was a gay experiment. Rigby wasn't his boyfriend.

Brennan repeated that point over and over again inside his head.

Rigby was not his boyfriend. He had no right to be upset just because Rigby was going out to get laid with some girl.

Brennan sighed and flopped down on the bed. Staring up at the ceiling, he fell to daydreaming. Maybe, for once in his life, Rigby would strike out with a girl. Maybe he would come home to Brennan and he'd want to tick something off the list after all. It wasn't beyond the realm of possibilities.

No! Brennan flung himself back onto his feet the moment he realised that if he was there when Rigby came home, even knowing Rigby's first choice was a woman, he would go crawling to Rigby anyway, happy to do whatever his friend wanted.

No, Brennan told himself again, only a fraction more calmly. He was not going to be a backup plan for a straight guy. He might be submissive, but he still had more pride than that. And he was not going to sit and mope either.

Rigby had the right attitude. A to do list wasn't a lifetime commitment. They hadn't made any promises of monogamy. There was no reason why Brennan couldn't go out and have some fun too.

He glanced at his watch. It was still early. He could make it into the city and hit a club or two. Throwing on a clean pair black jeans and his favourite blue shirt, he was out of the room in minutes. Slamming the door behind him, he put all thoughts of Rigby out of his head.

* * * *

"Can I buy you a drink?"

Brennan forced a smile. The guy was cute in his way, but Brennan never had preferred blonds. He wanted someone dark. He made his polite excuses and the guy walked away.

The next guy to approach him was as dark as Brennan could ever have wished for. If he'd been four inches taller, Brennan was sure they would have been able to have some fun together. Most nights the fact that Brennan was an inch or two taller than his partner wouldn't have mattered, but for some reason that night it did.

That night, no one was quite suitable for Brennan's mood, no one was quite close enough to his type to appeal to him. He didn't think he was being unrealistic in his expectations. All he wanted was someone who was tall and dark, with brown eyes, and a rich, deep voice, and a dominant attitude, and... Brennan sighed to himself. All he wanted was someone who looked, and sounded, and acted exactly like Rigby.

He frowned into his beer. No, that was wrong too. He wanted someone who was *almost* exactly like Rigby. Brennan wanted someone who was like Rigby, but who didn't have his friend's preference for women. He wanted the gay version of his straight best friend, and that night, in that club, no one was coming close.

"Boyfriend trouble?" the bartender asked.

Brennan looked across at him. If he'd had brown eyes instead of blue, he might have been close enough to take Rigby's place, but his eyes were wrong. Even if they picked a position where they'd never see each other's faces, Brennan knew he couldn't settle for blue eyes right then.

He hazily realised the man had asked him something and he was still waiting for an answer. "Pardon?"

"You've brushed off at least a dozen very hot men since you sat down on that bar stool," the bar man said. "Either you're incredibly fussy or your thoughts are on a guy who's not here."

Brennan felt a blush rise to his cheeks. He sent up silent thanks that Rigby apparently couldn't read him as well as a stranger could. "He's not my boyfriend," he muttered.

"And that's the trouble?" the bartender guessed.

"He's straight."

"Oh…" The bartender nodded, as if he'd heard it all before. Brennan guessed he probably had.

He rolled his eyes at himself. "I'm a gay man, in a gay bar, surrounded by other gay men. Why am I spending all my time thinking about a straight guy who's probably screwing some girl called Alice as we speak?" he asked the bartender.

The other man chose not to comment on that. He made a tactical retreat to the other end of the bar and served someone else. Brennan finished his drink and stared at the empty glass for a while.

The bartender came back. "Look at it this way," he offered. "The guy's probably a really bad lay. He's probably so used to girls he wouldn't know how to give a guy a good time."

Brennan didn't look up from his glass. "He gave me the best orgasm of my life, and it was only a hand job."

"This is still the straight guy we're talking about," the bartender checked.

Brennan nodded.

"The guy who doesn't like guys is the same guy who's playing with your cock?" he clarified.

Brennan nodded again, he looked up and saw the bartender's confused expression. "It's complicated," he said.

The bartender nodded. "Sounds it."

"I'm in love with him, and he's my best friend, and I really can't find anyone else who I want to have sex with, and..." he trailed off. "And I think I really need another drink."

Chapter Three

"You're drunk."

Brennan nodded. He wasn't actually so drunk he'd forgotten he was completely sloshed.

"It's two o'clock in the morning," Rigby added.

Brennan peered at his watch. "Yep," he agreed cheerfully. "Two o'clock." Even after everything that was going wrong in his world, he wasn't too drunk to tell the time. Brennan felt he had every right to feel very proud of himself for that.

Rigby got out of bed. He was only wearing his boxers. Brennan stared until he remembered he wasn't supposed to. Then he snapped his gaze back up to Rigby's face. His friend looked really pissed off.

"How was Alice?" Brennan asked.

"Who?"

Brennan frowned. "Your date. Alice." He scanned through beer fuddled memories. Rigby had definitely said her name was Alice something-or-other.

Rigby shook his head and started to undo the buttons on Brennan's shirt.

"What are you doing?" Brennan asked, watching the little bits of plastic slip through the holes.

"Undressing you," Rigby said, simply.

"You struck out with Alice?" Brennan realised. He'd been right to day dream about being an acceptable second choice.

"What are you on about now?" his friend asked.

"It's not nice to use your friend as a back up plan," Brennan mumbled, swatting Rigby's hands away as his friend undid the last button on his shirt.

It was especially cruel of Rigby not to tell him he was going use to him as a back up in advance. If he'd known, he could have stayed in and waited for him, or at least gone out but stayed sober enough to be of some use to his friend when he got home.

"How much did you have to drink?" Rigby asked him.

Brennan shrugged. "If you'd had the sense to tell me you might want to screw me, I would have drunk a lot less," he said, hating that he wasn't sober enough to keep the pouting tone out of his voice.

Rigby tucked a knuckle under his chin. He studied his eyes. Brennan looked up at the person he'd wanted to walk up to him in the bar all night.

"You're not making any sense," Rigby told him gently.

"You said you were going out with someone called Alice..." brain cells swam through the beer and finally clicked into place. "You said you were going to hook up with Alice Walker," he began to recount more confidently.

Rigby shook his head. "Stop talking, Bren. You're drunk and you're not making any sense."

Brennan shook his head. "You did say that." Through the vapour of alcoholic numbness he knew he still sounded like he was pouting.

Rigby's lips twitched into a smile. He took Brennan's shirt off.

"Why are you doing that?" Brennan asked, automatically cooperating with his friend even as he frowned at him.

"I'm taking your clothes off and putting you to bed."

"Oh…" Brennan watched Rigby undo his jeans. "Why?"

"Because if I put you to bed wearing all this, you'll spend the whole night wriggling and I won't get any sleep."

"That makes sense," Brennan allowed.

Rigby chuckled. "Now I know your paralytic. You only ever agree with me this easily when you're really drunk."

He seemed to hesitate when he realised Brennan was going commando under his jeans. The hesitation only lasted a moment. Then he pushed Brennan's jeans down.

Sitting Brennan on the edge of the bed, Rigby took off his shoes and socks and tossed all the clothes to one side of the room. Brennan watched everything he'd been wearing settle into a mess on the carpet. He tried to work out if he was allowed to complain about clothes being strewn all over the floor if they were his clothes.

"Stand up." Rigby pulled Brennan to his feet.

Brennan did as he was told. Standing naked in the middle of the room, he watched as Rigby turned down his blankets.

"Come on, in you get."

Brennan got into bed. Rigby guided him along every inch of the way as if he wasn't sure Brennan could cope on his own right then. "You don't have to do this," Brennan said, for form's sake. "I'm just drunk, not stupid."

Rigby took no notice. He pulled the blankets up and tucked his friend in. Brennan looked up and watched Rigby fuss over him.

"I'm sorry you didn't get laid," he offered.

Rigby chuckled. "Get some sleep. We can talk in the morning."

Brennan nodded. He turned his head on the pillow and watched Rigby get into bed. A few moments later, Rigby turned off the light and the room went dark. As sleepy as he felt, Brennan couldn't actually fall asleep. He turned his back to the room and curled into a comfortable little ball, but the position failed to help him block out the world and drift off.

He should have stayed in the room. The thought echoed around and around inside his head. He should have stayed in their room and waited for Rigby to come back. He should have waited just in case.

It was stupid to rush off just because it hurt his pride that Rigby might only screw him as a back up after his heterosexual plans fell through. If that was all he could get off Rigby, he should have taken it and held onto it as tight as he possibly could, because as much as his pride hurt at the idea of never being Rigby's first choice, it didn't hurt as much as the idea he'd screwed up his one chance to be there when Rigby might have wanted him. Who knew how long it would be before Rigby struck out again? With his track record, it might never happen again.

Brennan closed his eyes very tight. It was just the beer. It always did funny things to his head. It was just the beer that made him want to hide his head under his pillow and cry.

* * * *

"How's your head?"

Brennan glanced across the room at Rigby. His head felt fine until he remembered how much a fool he'd made of himself the previous night.

"I'm fine," he said. He took a deep breath. "About last night…"

"You were completely out of it," Rigby observed with obvious amusement.

"Yeah," Brennan agreed, clutching onto the idea with both hands, "so if I said anything weird…"

Rigby laughed. "You went on about me screwing Alice Walker and then you started mumbling something about me choosing to screw rather than get drunk or something."

"Oh…" Brennan said. He rubbed his head, which was actually getting more sore by the minute. "I didn't say anything about…" He nodded to himself. If he hadn't babbled anything coherent about not wanting to be Rigby's second choice, it was possible he hadn't screwed this up.

"What are you doing tonight?" Rigby asked him.

Brennan looked down. As much as he hated to admit it, even to himself, he was going to hang around in their room just in case Rigby struck out with whatever girl he had lined up for that night. He was going to sit around twiddling his thumbs in case his best friend decided he wanted to tick something off his gay to do list.

Realising Rigby was still waiting for an answer, Brennan mumbled something about finishing off an essay.

* * * *

Rigby tried to concentrate on his essay. It was impossible. The idea of working on something which didn't need to be handed in the next day went against his whole approach to the educational system. He had tomorrow to finish his thoughts on *The Color Purple*. Behind him the familiar sound of Brennan's fingers flying over his keyboard echoed in the overly quiet room. Rigby tapped his pen on his note pad.

The key in his pocket weighed heavily on his mind. Rigby took it out. He considered it for a few minutes, turning it over and over in his fingers. The silver metal caught the light. Rigby held back a frustrated sigh. Brennan was taking forever.

The longer he sat at his desk staring into space, the longer he had to spend thinking about what Brennan might have got up to the night before. Not only did he come back far too late and far too drunk for them to enjoy ticking something else off the list, but he'd obviously...

Rigby took a deep breath and forced himself to think about the whole situation calmly. Brennan had obviously gone out to get laid. He wouldn't have gone commando otherwise.

For a few minutes, his thoughts went off in another direction. Brennan going commando was, Rigby tried to think of another word, but the one he kept coming back to was, hot. The idea that he could slide his hand past the waist band of Brennan's jeans and there would be nothing blocking his access to his skin, to his cock, was incredible.

Other men being able to do the same thing was just wrong. Another man's hands on Brennan was not acceptable. Rigby frowned at the notice board hanging on the wall in front of him and pushed the distasteful image out of his head.

"When's your essay due in?" Rigby asked his friend. The sudden words sounded very loud in the quiet of the room.

If his essay wasn't due until tomorrow afternoon he just might be able to convince Brennan to play hooky for a while tonight and finish it in the morning.

Brennan didn't even slow down the rapid click of keys. "Next Wednesday."

Rigby sat up straight in his chair. "What?"

"It's due in next Wednesday," Brennan repeated distractedly.

To hell with that! "Come on, we're going out."

"I still have half of it left to do," Brennan protested.

"And almost a week to do it!" Throwing Brennan's coat across to him, Rigby pulled his jacket on. "Save what you've done and start moving." He hadn't had any fun with Brennan last night, he wasn't going to waste another night.

"It's gone midnight," Brennan pointed out.

"Exactly. It's far too late to study now. It's probably bad for your brain." It was also incredibly inconsistent for a man who'd rolled in at two that morning.

"Where do you want to go?"

Rigby tossed the key in the air and caught it as he walked out of the room. "Stop dawdling, Bren."

As Brennan finally got moving and closed down his lap top, Rigby headed for the stairs.

"Where are we going?" Brennan asked, closing their bedroom door and hurrying to catch up with him.

Rigby kept walking. "To tick something off a list."

"*The* list?" Brennan asked.

"Yeah." Like there was another list.

"I thought you wouldn't want to after..." he trailed off. "I mean... um... which thing do you want to tick off?"

Rigby turned the corner and the sports hall came into view along with the swimming pool building.

Brennan stopped walking. "You want to go skinny dipping?" he asked.

"That's the idea." Rigby didn't bother to stop walking. Brennan always caught up sooner or later.

"You want us to break into university property?" Brennan specified, as he made it back to Rigby's side, he didn't seem overly impressed with the idea. "Maybe you'd actually prefer us to go back to our room and do one of the other — "

"Angela works there as a life guard," Rigby cut in. "She had a key."

"And you stole her key? Rig, she's going to kill you!"

Brennan sounded so appalled, Rigby couldn't hold back a chuckle. "I didn't steal it. I borrowed it."

"And she's okay with this?"

"She gave me the key."

"Are there any of your ex-girlfriends who don't jump when you call?" Brennan demanded suddenly, as they reached the side door into the swimming pool.

"What can I say, I'm a nice guy..." Rigby slid the key into the lock and pushed the door open.

The smell of chlorine flooded out of the building.

Brennan hesitated.

"Come on," Rigby coaxed, "it's not breaking and entering if we have a key, is it?"

Brennan stepped inside. He reached for the switch to turn on the over head lights.

Rigby covered Brennan's hand. "You don't really get the theory of sneaking around, do you?"

Brennan shrugged and dropped his hand back to his side. "You've always been the sneaky one."

"I thought you said you've done this before."

"Skinny dipping, not sneaking. You can do one without the other."

"When?"

"In the reservoir when we went camping in the last year of school."

"With who?" Rigby said. Frowning over his shoulder at Brennan, he led the way to the pool. He didn't remember any skinny dipping trips.

"George Knight."

An image sprung to Rigby's mind of the boy in school with them. On that particular camping trip

George would have been eighteen, the same as the rest of them. Tall and blond, the guy thought he was a walking, talking gift from God. A horrible thought occurred to Rigby. "He's gay?"

Brennan nodded and stared over the water when they reached the edge of the pool.

Rigby's frown deepened. "You and him got it together?"

Brennan nodded again, he seemed fascinated by the ripples on the surface of the water. He pushed his hands deep into the pockets of his jacket as if the room was cold rather than balmy.

"You and George Knight?" Rigby demanded.

"Yeah," Brennan said, "why not?"

"Besides the obvious point of because he's a complete bastard?" Rigby asked.

Brennan glanced across to him.

"Well?" Rigby prompted.

Brennan shrugged. "He's not the nicest guy in the world — he's not the worst guy either."

"He's probably the kind of man who enjoys holding someone's head under the water just to see how long it takes them to drown. He's not the kind of guy anyone in their right mind goes wandering off with in the middle of the night to go swimming," Rigby said.

"The swimming wasn't really the main attraction."

Rigby clenched his jaw. He took a deep breath. He'd never had any problem discussing Brennan's sex life — Brennan was the only one who ever blushed. If Brennan wanted to screw guys, Rigby didn't have a problem with that, but he'd assumed his friend had the sense to pick the right guy. The thought of him with George Knight made Rigby's skin crawl. "You should have told me."

"Told you what?" Brennan asked.

"About you and George."

"Why?" He seemed genuinely confused by the idea. As if it wasn't obvious.

"I could have looked out for you," Rigby told him.

Brennan raised an eyebrow at him. "I didn't know voyeurism was on your to do list."

Rigby gritted his teeth. "Watching wasn't what I had in mind."

His friend's lips twitched into a smile. "You really take your experimentation seriously don't you, Rig? I'd been screwing my way around the clubs for months before I tried out a threesome."

"A what?" Picturing Brennan with two guys wasn't an improvement on the pictures already racing through Rigby's head. He looked across at his friend. Everything Brennan had said that evening contained a very Brennan like comment. But there was something off about the delivery, it felt like every sarcastic word was forced and calculated rather than springing naturally, just from Brennan being Brennan.

"A threesome," Brennan explained patiently, in that same slightly wrong tone of voice. "It's when three guys get together to have sex, it usually involves giving one guy a blow job while another guy – "

"I know what a threesome is," Rigby snapped. "Who were they?"

"You don't know them."

Rigby turned his attention to the water, no longer able to look at Brennan without seeing him in a situation he didn't like. "Did you know them?" he asked.

"No, not really," Brennan admitted. "Not beyond what we did together that night."

"So you just jump into bed with anyone?" Rigby demanded.

"There wasn't a bed involved in that particular case," Brennan corrected, "just a wall in a club."

Rigby shook his head. When he looked back across to Brennan his friend was watching him with a curious expression.

"I'm no more a slut than you are, Rig," he said softly.

Rigby turned his attention once more to the water. "I never said you were a slut." Brennan was better than that. He might not act like he was better than that, he certainly hadn't acted better than that wherever he went commando to the previous night, but Rigby knew he was.

"You really think your mind's a mystery to me?" Brennan smiled to himself. "I know what you're thinking, Rig. You think different rules apply to me than to you, that the fact I don't bother to find out a guy's mother's maiden name and star sign before we have some fun makes me a slut. Well, so what if I am? I find out the important things. If he's legal and up for it, who am I hurting? Anyway, it's not as if I'm dating someone who cares who I have sex with, is it?"

Rigby frowned. Brennan deserved better than cheap screws in the back room of clubs. He deserved… Rigby glanced across the room at his friend. Brennan deserved better than once around a to do list, as well.

He looked away and shrugged out of his coat. "Are we going to do this, or not?" Rigby demanded. Coat tossed to the wall, Rigby pulled his t-shirt over his head.

Brennan glanced at him, then he looked quickly back to the pool.

Rigby waited a few seconds to see if Brennan was going to get with the programme. When it became obvious Brennan wasn't in any sort of hurry, Rigby stopped undressing for a moment. "Remember when we did the lifesaving course with school?" he asked.

Brennan nodded.

"Remember the bit where we had to swim three lengths fully clothed?"

Brennan half nodded, then he caught up with where the conversation was heading. He took his coat off.

Rigby smiled. Maybe Brennan did know what he was thinking after all.

Kicking off his shoes and socks, Rigby dispensed with his jeans and his boxers in a few brisk movements. Brennan wasn't in quite such a rush. Rigby kept his patience until Brennan was down to his boxers and socks. It seemed like a calculated insult that Brennan should go commando for other guys and then put his boxers on to go out with him.

When Brennan stood near the edge for several long seconds, making no attempt to hurry it up and get back to commando status, Rigby was done with waiting. He wrapped his arm around Brennan's waist and jumped in the pool.

Brennan spluttered and pushed his hair out of his eyes, fighting his way back to the surface. "You…!"

"I told you to hurry up," Rigby pointed out, entirely unrepentant as he swam into the middle of the pool.

Brennan swam back to the edge. "Jackass."

Rigby trod water, watching as his friend held onto the side and finally got around to dropping his boxers and socks on the side of the pool.

Rigby grinned. "You know, you were right about one thing. You can't be that much of a slut if it takes a guy this much trouble to get you naked," he called across the water.

"And somehow you are still on speaking terms with all your ex-girlfriends?" Brennan muttered.

"I must be doing something they like," Rigby shot back. "If you stop moping I might show you what that something is later."

Brennan shook his head, but the smile that had been absent all day slowly came back. Rigby loved that smile. It always told him that Brennan had forgiven him and he was pretty happy with life in general. It felt like Brennan had pushed aside whatever was bothering him all day and they were back to being the way they had always been with each other.

Pushing away from the side, Brennan started to swim. He slid through the water leaving hardly a ripple in his wake. Diving down and spinning under the water at the far end of the pool Brennan raced back down the length of the pool.

Rigby spread his arms on the edge of the pool, leaned back and enjoyed the view. Brennan looked amazing, it was as if the water made him sparkle. Rigby shook his head. For a guy—Brennan looked amazing *for a guy*. He looked amazing in a way which meant Rigby could understand why a gay man would be attracted to him. He cleared his throat, pleased he'd unravelled that thought to his own satisfaction.

He watched Brennan take another length in a matter of seconds. If he was gay, Rigby decided, he would definitely want to get it together with Brennan. Apparently, it wasn't that difficult to get him to agree to a casual hook up. Rigby shifted his arms along the length of the wall, unable to find an entirely comfortable position. Just because he'd agreed to go through the list with him, that didn't mean Brennan should go along with other people's plans just as easily.

Of course he knew Brennan went out and got laid. He didn't think his best friend was a virgin. Still, the idea of Brennan falling into bed with whoever clicked his fingers and bought him a drink made Rigby want to pull Brennan close and never let him out of his sight ever again. The idea that someone could have taken advantage of Brennan when he was drunk out of his skull made Rigby's stomach knot up.

And George Knight! He was a vicious little sod to the world in general. Rigby could guess how he'd treat a lover. Rigby frowned. Brennan shouldn't be with someone like that. Brennan was a gentle soul. He wouldn't know how to stand up to someone who just wanted a cheap lay. He wouldn't know how to insist that someone treat him better.

Brennan needed someone who would look after him.

Rigby ran a hand through his hair, pushing the dark, wet strands back from his face. He hadn't been doing a good enough job with that. He'd have to start keeping a closer eye on his friend. He shouldn't have backed off and let him have some space just because he blushed when Rigby asked him about his sex life.

He'd been looking after Brennan since the first day in school. He wasn't going to stop now. Brennan was his.

Water fountained up as Brennan made another turn right next to Rigby's side.

"What the..." Rigby spluttered, wiping the water out of his eyes.

Brennan trod water in the centre of the pool and laughed.

"Declaring war?" Rigby asked.

Brennan's eyes opened very wide. He dove away to the left. Rigby splashed after him. He didn't have his friend's grace in the water—but he had more muscle and a better understanding of tactics. He finally cornered Brennan in the deep end of the pool. Putting his hand on the ledge either side of him, he trapped him there. Brennan smiled and ducked under his arm before Rigby could think to block the space under the water.

As he turned to give chase, Brennan stretched his arms out and put them on either edge, as if he really thought he could out muscle Rigby if it came down to it.

Rigby grinned and let Brennan go on thinking that for a while. "And now you've got me, what are you going to do with me?"

Brennan hesitated for a briefest moment. It almost looked like he hadn't realised they were working their way towards ticking something else off the list.

Then he matched Rigby's grin and disappeared under the water again. A second later Rigby felt

Brennan's lips wrap around his cock. He really hoped the water swirling over Brennan's head kept his embarrassingly high pitched yelp from reaching his ears.

Air bubbled from Brennan's mouth and rushed against his shaft. His friend's tongue teased his foreskin. Rigby gripped the wall tighter as Brennan took his rapidly stiffening cock into his mouth for the first time. Hot suction surrounded him. Rigby looked down through the distortion of the water and watched Brennan begin to bob his head, taking his cock deeper into his mouth with every movement.

His hair floated out from his head in a blond wavy cloud. His eyes were scrunched up shut tight against the water. He still looked perfect.

Steadying himself with his hands on Rigby's waist, Brennan's legs kicked out behind him in the deep water, keeping him level. Rigby rested back against the wall. He looked along Brennan's body, over the lean muscles in his back, down to the tight buttocks. For the first time he got why mermen were the stuff of fantasies.

Thirty seconds later Rigby frowned. Brennan had always been a great swimmer but there was a line between as erotic as hell and just damn crazy. Brennan had swum straight past that line without a second thought.

Grabbing Brennan's arm, Rigby pulled him up to the surface. Brennan gasped for air and spat out a mouthful of chlorine and water. Rigby held him steady as he grappled for the side.

"Are you trying to drown yourself?" Rigby demanded, pushing Brennan's hair back from his eyes and pulling the slightly smaller man close into his body so he was safe where Rigby could keep hold of him.

Brennan smiled as he blinked the water out of his eyes. "I'm fine."

Rigby's frown stayed where it was. "Just when were you going to come back up?"

Brennan shrugged.

Rigby shook his head. "You have no survival instinct, do you?"

Brennan didn't bother to answer. He tapped the edge of the pool. "Sit up here and I'll finish you off without you having to worry about my lung capacity."

On the one hand, Rigby knew Brennan was his and that obviously made him responsible for Brennan's safety. On the other hand a blow job was a blow job and not to be turned down lightly. Rigby pushed himself up onto the ledge in one easy movement, water cascading off his body.

Brennan nudged his knees apart and hooked his elbows on the outside of his spread legs to keep his head and shoulders out of the water. Rigby's cock stood to attention just an inch away from his lips.

Rigby studied their position. Brennan looked secure. He wouldn't slip back into the water while Rigby had his attention elsewhere. Taking Brennan by the arms he shifted until they were closer still and Brennan was well within catching distance should Rigby need to pull him out of the water.

Brennan took the head of Rigby's cock in his mouth.

Rigby shifted his hips but he couldn't thrust into the warm, wet cocoon without risking them both toppling into the water. He had no choice but to stay still and let Brennan set the pace and do exactly what he wanted with him.

All he could do was watch. Brennan's lips wrapped tight around his shaft, a pale pink line against hard, flushed arousal. Rigby watched fascinated as he disappeared again and again into Brennan's hot, slick mouth.

Nothing a man could do to him should feel so wonderful, but it did. It felt better than anything he remembered with any of his female partners. Brennan had serious skills, but just as much as flickering tongued expertise, Rigby couldn't push away the fact this was Brennan. This was the guy he played rugby with, shared his first beer with, and got into so much trouble with as they grew up. It was Brennan Talbot who had his lips wrapped ever so snugly around his cock. It was his Brennan.

His Brennan, the guy who was always part of the backdrop to his life, was suddenly changing into someone new and confusing. Into someone who'd done things Rigby never tried, someone who knew how to make him moan low in the back of his throat and someone who might somehow be more to him than just a friend.

Chapter Four

Brennan slid his hands up Rigby's hips and settled them on his bare buttocks. He just wanted to make sure he didn't slide backwards into the water at a bad moment. No one ever wanted their lover to stop when it was going good—your lover almost drowning had to spoil the moment. He wasn't really taking advantage of the situation to sneak in a bit of contact that wasn't specified on the list.

He bobbed his head over Rigby's lap, taking his erection a little deeper into his mouth. It was tempting to keep a few tricks back and suggest they be added to the list as separate to do points, but he desperately needed to make a good impression.

He wanted Rigby to compare him to all the girls he'd ever screwed and realise Brennan could hold his own against any of them. He wanted to become Rigby's first choice of sexual partner. And more than anything, he wanted Rigby to regret only deciding to doing everything once, because if Rigby wanted to come back for more then…

Brennan closed his eyes. Straight. That was the important thing to remember. Rigby wasn't his lover, not really, and he certainly wasn't his boyfriend. There would be no civil commitment ceremony. There would be no two point four adopted children. There would be no happily ever after for him and Rigby. There would be no doing anything more than once.

He had to be realistic and take what he could get. He could be the experiment Rigby enjoyed for a while—a good memory for his friend to look back on after he started screwing women again, because he was never going to be Rigby's first choice.

Brennan lapped delicately at the tip of Rigby's cock, spreading the flavour over his tongue. Pre-cum was a huge improvement on chlorine. Brennan swirled his tongue as he lowered his head again.

Rigby's grip on his arm tightened. Brennan smiled to himself. His lips wrapped tight around Rigby's cock. His cheeks hollowed and he created a perfect vacuum. Rigby actually possessed far better manners than Brennan expected. There was no rushing him to speed it along, even though Rigby was definitely enjoying himself. Every muscle in Rigby's body was riddled with tension as he fought to keep still. Contrary to all Brennan's expectations, Rigby was being nice, regardless of his own frustration.

Brennan pushed further forward until the tip of Rigby's cock slid into his throat. Rigby moaned above him. He released one of Brennan's arms and placed his hand on the back of Brennan's head.

It was Rigby. Brennan pushed away how much he always hated it when guys did that. It was Rigby, and his friend wouldn't try to keep him where he didn't want to be. Brennan carefully tested the strength of his hold on his hair.

As he expected, Rigby's hand moved with his head, not applying any pressure, just being there. Brennan relaxed. He wondered if he was more used to screwing guys like Rigby rather than strangers in clubs, if he could get used to the close comforting feel of a man's hand on the back of his head when he went down on them.

Except Brennan knew he wasn't going to get used to it. He stilled with Rigby's cock buried deep inside his mouth. For a few long seconds he just enjoyed the feel of Rigby stretching his lips and filling him up. He memorised every detail, then he brought himself back to reality.

Comfortable though the pool was, it was approaching two o'clock in the morning. They couldn't stay there all night. Brennan began to work Rigby's erection in earnest, taking him deep into his throat in a punishing rhythm.

"Gonna come." Rigby whispered the warning. His voice was hoarse and deep and the most perfect thing Brennan ever heard.

Brennan kept doing what he was doing until Rigby's hips bucked. His hand tightened in Brennan's hair, holding him close as he spilled into his mouth. Swallowing rapidly, Brennan took everything his friend could give him, savouring every drop because he knew he'd never taste Rigby again.

Sucking gently while Rigby softened in his mouth, Brennan looked up and watched Rigby slowly pull his thoughts together. His grip on his arm and his hair eased slowly, as if he was afraid Brennan would slide if not held close. He clumsily stroked Brennan's hair back flat, patting him on the head before he returned his grip to his arm.

Brennan reluctantly let Rigby's cock slip from his mouth. He licked his lips, enjoying a last little stolen taste. Now all he needed to do was lighten the mood and let Rigby off the hook for returning the favour, because if Rigby got the impression he expected the same in return, Rigby wouldn't want to tick anything at all off his list ever again. Brennan gave a mental sigh. It wasn't easy to come up with friendly banter when all he really wanted to do was come.

Water swirled around his erection, torturing him with a warm wet sensation which offered far too little stimulation and no prospect at all of release. Still smiling, because even if he didn't get to come, he'd just gone down on his wet dream, Brennan looked up and met Rigby's eyes. He smiled back. Brennan's smile grew. He'd put that smile on his friend's face.

A door banged somewhere in the building.

Brennan turned to see where the noise came from. Rigby didn't bother. He scrambled back, pulling Brennan out of the pool with him. Scooping up their clothes, he dragged Brennan behind a partition leading to the diving pool.

Footsteps echoed through the swimming hall. Brennan leaned against the partition and tried to catch his breath. Rigby peeped around the edge of the dividing panels as the footsteps came closer. Security guard, he mouthed to Brennan.

Lifting his eyes to the heavens, Brennan really hoped someone was listening, because if they weren't he was going to get arrested. Worse, Rigby was going to get arrested with him. While a gay guy might be able to pass off getting cautioned for indecent exposure with one of the hottest men in the university like it was some sort of amusing anecdote, a straight guy was going to have a hell of a lot of trouble explaining why there weren't any girls there with them.

Brennan listened to the guard walk around the room, whistling under his breath. He was sure the heavy footsteps got closer and closer each second. The guard would have to see the marks where they'd splashed water around the edge of the pool. He'd have to see two sets of footprints lead behind the panel.

Brennan closed his eyes. Rigby kissed him.

He grabbed Rigby's arms, so shocked he wasn't immediately sure if he wanted to pull him close or push him away. Then he came to his senses and pulled Rigby close. If they got arrested this would inevitably mark the end of Rigby's gay experiment. He should make the most of their last kiss.

His erection curved up towards his stomach, trapped between them. Rigby didn't seem to mind another guy's hard on pressed against his naked body. Brennan rocked his hips against his pool slick skin. Rigby's tongue slid into his mouth and Rigby murmured his approval.

Brennan tensed. They were going to give away their location. Rigby's hands dropped to his arse and pulled him closer actually encouraging him to rub up against his body. Brennan didn't need to be invited twice. He moaned louder than Rigby ever did because for a few moments it felt like he was the only person in the world that Rigby wanted to have sex with. It felt like he was Rigby's first choice for everything.

When Rigby broke the kiss, Brennan remembered he was supposed to be pissed off with Rigby for some reason other than Rigby stopping kissing him. He forced himself to shoot an accusing look at his friend.

Rigby chuckled. "He's gone," he said, so loud, the words seemed to echo around the room.

"What?" Brennan whispered, looking over Rigby's shoulder.

"The guard left."

"When?"

"Just before I kissed you."

Brennan looked around the partition. "You could have told me!" he hissed.

"You can stop whispering now."

Brennan shot him a look to show just how unamused he was by Rigby's flippant attitude. Rigby grinned. Brennan shook his head and bit back his own smile. He started picking through the pile of clothes Rigby scooped up and sorting out whose was whose. "I thought you'd crossed kissing off your list, anyway?" he said.

Rigby grabbed his wrist as Brennan picked up a pair of jeans.

Brennan looked up at him.

"Do you have any objection to me kissing you?" Rigby demanded.

Brennan swallowed and looked back at the jeans in his hand. Of course he didn't. He shook his head. If he had his way Rigby would keep kissing him forever.

Rigby seemed to wait for an answer.

"No objection," Brennan whispered, hoping Rigby didn't hear in his voice just how true that was.

Rigby ran his finger tip along Brennan's lips. They parted for him without any instruction from his brain.

"You give really great head," Rigby observed.

Brennan nodded and stored the idle compliment in the back of his mind to be savoured later.

"And you let me come in your mouth." Rigby's finger traced the line around his lips again. "I've never done that before."

Brennan blinked at him. He frowned, wondering what punch line Rigby was working his way towards. He pulled away from Rigby's touch and went back to sorting through their clothes. "You're hardly a virgin."

"Either they wanted to use condoms or they stopped before spit or swallow became an issue." The way Rigby said it made it sound like the truth.

Brennan hesitated, glancing back to his friend.

"I've never kissed someone and tasted myself in their mouth," Rigby mentioned casually, taking his jeans out of Brennan's hand and swapping them for Brennan's.

Brennan licked his lips. He'd swear he could still taste Rigby there now. "Another thing for your list," he said.

Rigby smiled. "Yeah, I guess it is."

Stupidly, Brennan felt a blush rise to his cheeks. He really could give Rigby something his ex-girlfriends couldn't. He turned away to start pulling his t-shirt on, wondering if letting Rigby do things that girls wouldn't agree to automatically made him Rigby's first choice for those things.

"Aren't you forgetting something?"

Brennan sorted through the clothes, looking for his boxers. "Like what?"

"Like this?" Rigby stroked his fingers along Brennan's erection.

Instinct made him thrust into the contact. A noise outside made him freeze.

"No, let's just get out of here before we get caught." That was good. That would let Rigby off the hook. Brennan was impressed with himself—he actually sounded like he thought not getting off was a good idea.

Rigby didn't look entirely impressed, but after a few moments he nodded his agreement and dropped his hand away.

Brennan looked through the clothes again. He looked at the floor around them. To the left he saw the soggy little pile of boxers and socks he'd taken off while already in the pool. Picking them up, he glanced regretfully at them and tossed them in a rubbish bin hanging on the wall nearby.

He pulled his jeans, the denim sticking to his damp skin every inch of the way. He did his best to tuck his erection comfortably away as he did up the zip. Behind him, he heard Rigby pulling on his clothes. A low wooden bench ran down the side of the wall.

Brennan sat down and looked at his shoes with a distinct lack of enthusiasm. He'd got used to going commando when he went to clubs, but he'd always hated the feel of shoes without socks and nothing was ever going to change that. A small bundle of material hit his shoulder. Brennan caught the pair of socks.

He frowned at them. Who the hell carried a spare of socks with him when he went skinny dipping? He looked across at Rigby and dropped his gaze to his friend's feet. "What are you going to wear?"

Rigby pulled one of his trainers over his bare skin and started to do the laces up. "Doesn't bother me."

Brennan hesitated. "It doesn't bother me either."

Rigby pulled his other shoe on, not taking the least bit of notice of the lie.

Brennan undid the socks from the aerodynamic ball Rigby had rolled them into and slipped them onto his feet. Pulling his shoes on, he wriggled his toes. Wriggling into his clothes on while he was still damp from the pool wasn't one of his favourite things, but the dry socks were a nice touch.

He grabbed his coat and put it on as Rigby did the same. They walked out of the pool hall in silence. As Rigby closed the door and locked it behind them, Brennan pushed his hands into his pockets. It was a clear, cloudless night. The early hour of the morning left frost covering the grass.

Brennan looked down at his feet most of the way home, watching his shoes crunch through the thin frost as they took a shortcut over the grassed area. Brennan looked at his feet in Rigby's socks. It was just like his friend, doing something daft without thinking about the consequences, then making up for it afterwards with some silly little gesture. It always made Brennan wonder just how much of a romantic his friend was with the women in his life.

When he finally found a girl he wanted and settled down, Brennan was sure Rigby would end up being as soppy as hell with her. He was just the type of guy to run rings around the whole world then fall to his knees for his girl. His girl…

Brennan sighed to himself and walked a little quicker.

Rigby easily kept pace with him. He had a damn long, loping stride which ate up the ground in no time. Brennan had never been able to outpace him. He could just imagine some pretty little girl tottering alongside him in ridiculously high heels. A girl would never keep up with Rigby.

They turned the corner and Rigby let them into their hall of residence. Two flights of stairs later they stepped into their room. There was no way Brennan could slip straight back into being a best friend without a few moments to himself.

He grabbed his wash bag and his towel. "I'm going to go rinse the chlorine off."

The showers were only three doors down from their room. Brennan pulled off his clothes. Hitting the taps, he stepped under the spray the moment it warmed up. Brennan sighed. His erection had flourished through every frustrating step of the walk home. Checking the curtain separating him from the rest of the room was firmly in place, Brennan took his cock in his hand.

Rigby's rhythm called to him, tempting him away from everything he'd worked out for himself over the years. As his hand sped up, his mind turned to Rigby too. Picturing them back in the corner of the pool, he imagined what they could have done if they really were boyfriends, if Rigby liked men for something more than a list or a backup plan. He pictured what would have happened if he turned Rigby to face the side of the pool rather than told him to sit up on the edge.

Braced against the wall, Rigby would have looked stunning. With his hands on the edge of the pool, holding himself up in the water, he wouldn't have been able to do anything more than take what Brennan gave him. Brennan imagined sliding his hands over Rigby's back, slipping over the dripping muscles, teasing Rigby with the possibility of the position until he squirmed.

Brennan slid imaginary hands down Rigby's back and cupping his friend's beautiful arse in his palms. He'd be so tight and glorious to slide into, all slick and ready for him. Rigby would take him perfectly, because there was no way anything with Rigby could be anything less than perfect.

Brennan rested his forehead against the wet tiles lining the shower stall. He chuckled under his breath. Who was he kidding? Top or bottom, Rigby would be pushy and demanding and boss him around just the way he always did. And he'd love every minute of it, no matter how much sarcasm he used to hide his pleasure.

Brennan smiled as he changed the one size fits all fantasy into a real picture of him and Rigby together. Rigby's hands reaching behind and gripping his arse, demanding he take up the exact rhythm he wanted. Ordering Brennan to go harder, faster.

That was right, Rigby would like it rough and rapid, especially if he was bottoming. He'd never have any

patience with his own body, never give himself time
to relax and adjust. Everything always had to be now
with Rigby. If it hurt, he'd just keep going until he got
used to it.

He'd be different when he was topping. Rigby was
really used to girls. Brennan guessed you needed to be
really slow and gentle with a girl. He'd be like that at
first, until he realised Brennan wouldn't break.
Though there would still be a little bit of that in Rigby,
that complete certainty he was stronger than the
whole world so he had to look after everyone else.

Keeping up Rigby's demanding rhythm didn't give
Brennan much time to fantasise. Brennan came against
the shower tiles as his orgasm washed over him. He
leaned his head against the wall and watched the
water quickly rinse his semen away. His fantasy
version of Rigby drained away too, leaving Brennan to
go back to the one who actually preferred women.

Brennan lingered in the shower for a long time, not
quite sure what he would say to his friend when he
went back to the room. Finally drying himself off and
wrapping a towel around his waist he walked the few
paces back to their room.

Rigby looked him up and down as he stepped in.

Brennan turned to his wardrobe, telling himself to
just act like nothing had changed. It should be easy.
Nothing had changed. They'd gone swimming, they'd
fooled around, he'd sucked Rigby's cock and now
they were going to go to sleep.

"Nice shower?" Rigby asked.

"Yeah." Brennan grabbed a pair of pyjama bottoms
out of his wardrobe. He hesitated for a moment, but
he forced himself to act as naturally as he always did.

They'd never been shy around each other and now was a bloody stupid time to start being modest. Brennan dropped the towel and pulled the bottom half of his pyjamas on.

He slipped into his bed without meeting Rigby's eyes.

Curling into a small ball he held the realisation that Rigby still wanted him tight to his chest. Maybe he only wanted him for the purposes of the list. Maybe he was only a second choice, but he was something more than a friend to Rigby now, and that let him go to sleep with a smile on his face.

* * * *

Rigby glared at the list pinned up on his notice board. He didn't have much longer to work out his next move. He knew Brennan's routine better than he did his own and his friend would be back from his particle physics lecture any moment now.

What he didn't know, was what to do with Brennan now. Rigby was quite willing to admit he wasn't an expert on gay sex, but he'd always assumed there was some sort of reciprocation involved. Both people were supposed to get off on whatever two people did together. That was the whole point no matter which way you swung.

Rigby looked at the list again. Perhaps Brennan never had that part of the logic explained to him. As smart as he was, Brennan could be incredibly dopey about the strangest things.

He was too trusting and too innocent to look after himself. That was why he had Rigby. No matter how many men he'd screwed around with, he obviously hadn't found the kind of lovers who would make him feel he was more than someone to be used.

He was also becoming more and more convinced that something had happened that night Brennan got drunk. His friend hadn't been the same since that night.

But damn it, even before that, Rigby couldn't work out why Brennan didn't demand more from life than he was getting. He was a good guy — the best there was. He wasn't so self effacing that he didn't believe he deserved to be happy.

So why didn't he have a boyfriend? Why had he never even been with someone for long enough to mention them by name to his best friend? Sure, Brennan had needed to deal with the whole gay coming out thing, but he'd been out for years. He should be secure enough on the gay scene to find someone worth dating for more than a few hours.

Rigby rocked back on his chair and looked out of the window between their beds. He wasn't going to be part of that. He wasn't going to be someone else who just used Brennan. He wouldn't be someone who just got off then buggered off.

He stared out of the window until Brennan came home, right on schedule. Standing up, he stepped into the middle of the room, right into Brennan's path.

Brennan, reading as he walked, went straight into him.

Rigby easily kept him on his feet, holding onto both his arms and keeping him close. "Anything interesting?"

Brennan looked back at the flier for some sort of university event. "Not really." He looked up at Rigby. "What are you up to?"

"I was just waiting for you to come home."

Brennan turned away and put his bag on the chair by Rigby's desk.

Rigby traced his line of sight to the list on the notice board.

"You want to do something?" Brennan asked.

Rigby could think of a lot of things he would like to do with Brennan, a lot of them were things he hadn't known the words for when he wrote the damn list.

"Do you?" he fired back at Brennan.

"Whatever you want," Brennan said with a shrug, as if he didn't even think it was worth him having an opinion.

"What you want doesn't matter?" Rigby asked. That was exactly the sort of stupid idea he didn't want in Brennan's head. "What sort of bastards do you date?"

Brennan half smiled. "I usually date the convenient kind. And yes, what I want matters. But I'm versatile enough that I enjoy most things, so I'm pretty flexible about the details if you want to..."

"Convenient?" It was the only word that registered with Rigby.

Brennan shrugged again. "Yeah, they're convenient."

The horrible suspicion formed in Rigby's mind, for the first time he considered the possibility that Brennan wasn't being taken advantage of. "So the way you work your sex life, that's the way you want things?"

"I'm not sure I even understand the question." Brennan looked back to the flier he seemed so fascinated with.

"A different guy every time, once through a to do list and move on to someone else? You like living your life like that?"

Brennan didn't look back to him. "Why not?"

"Because maybe you want something better?" Rigby suggested. "Maybe you want someone who will be more to you than a quick screw against the wall?"

Brennan shook his head. "I'm not looking for more than what I have."

Rigby scrambled for another explanation. "So, you're waiting until you grow up before you think about settling down?"

Brennan gave a bitter laugh. "No, I'm not looking for more at any point. I don't want more than some quick fun from anyone I meet in a club."

Rigby felt anger boil up inside him. "So *everyone's* just a convenient screw to you?"

Brennan shrugged. "I always make it clear from the start. No harm, no foul."

Yes, he had. Once through the list. That was the deal. It hadn't occurred to Rigby that Brennan would ever want more from him, not until he suddenly realised he wanted far more from Brennan. "In that case, just forget it."

"Forget what?"

"This?" Rigby grabbed the list from his notice board. Crumpling it in his hand he tossed it towards the bin.

Brennan frowned, all his attention focused on the white paper ball on the floor, a strange, unreadable expression on his face.

Rigby ran his hand through his hair, trying to think sensibly, but he couldn't make sense of this mess. The only conclusion he could think of was Brennan wasn't the guy Rigby thought he knew, and he wasn't what Rigby wanted him to be.

"I thought you were better than this," Rigby muttered.

"Better than what?"

"Better than someone who can't give a damn about whoever he's with," Rigby threw at him.

"What?" Brennan asked softly.

"That is why, isn't it?" Rigby snapped. "That's why you always have one night stands instead of boyfriends?"

Brennan shook his head, brushing the issue aside. "Don't be a hypocrite, Rig. You've had your fair share of one night wonders too."

"Yes, I have. And I've had girlfriends, and people I care about, people I wanted to spend more than one night with. And yes, I do want more than any of that with some person at some point. I'm not so much of a slut that I don't want to settle down at some point."

"But you think that's what I am?" Brennan asked coolly.

"It sure as hell looks like it from here," Rigby flung at him.

Grabbing his bag, Brennan headed for the door. "I can't stick around to listen to this!"

Rigby stepped into his way.

Brennan shouldered into him, but Rigby was dammed if he would let Brennan walk away from him the way he walked away from every man he'd ever screwed. Rigby stood his ground, blocking Brennan's access to the door.

"Back off." Brennan tried to push him away. He only succeeded in pushing himself back into the middle of the room.

Rigby folded his arms. "Or what?"

Brennan took a deep breath and closed his eyes. "Don't do this to me, Rig," he pleaded. "Just let me be."

"No. If you have a problem with what I say, you deal with it. You don't walk away from me. If you don't like facing the truth, that's your problem."

"The truth?" Brennan snapped. "You really want to know the truth about why I put up with casual fucks in the back room of clubs?"

"Yes, please do share," Rigby shouted back, "because I'd really like to know what changed you from the guy I grew up with to someone I've never even met."

"You!" Brennan yelled. "Okay, Rig? You're the reason why I've never had a boyfriend. I go out and screw around, but I don't stick around afterwards because I come back to you. Every single damn time— I come back to you!"

"You…" Rigby tried to make sense of what Brennan said and failed.

"Are you happy now, Rig? Because that's the truth. Now let me pass."

Rigby stayed where he was.

Brennan tried to side step him. "Get out of my way."

Rigby shook his head. "No."

Brennan looked up at him. Their eyes met.

"You're in love with me," Rigby realised.

"No," Brennan said firmly.

Rigby caught his arm as Brennan tried to push past again.

"Let me go."

Rigby caught his face, and cupped it between his palms, forcing Brennan to meet his gaze again. "You're in love with me."

Brennan closed his eyes in a last defence, but he wasn't quick enough. Rigby saw the truth shining in his eyes.

Rigby stared down at his friend. "You're in love with me," he said again.

"Stop saying that," Brennan whispered.

Everything clicked into place. "That's why you kissed me," Rigby realised. "It's why you agreed to go along with this whole stupid idea with the list. Hell, I'll bet it's why you didn't even demand to get off in return."

"You're straight," Brennan whispered.

"And that means I'm only interested in what I could take from you…" Rigby closed his own eyes for a moment and rested his forehead against Brennan's. It was such Brennan like logic. His friend morphed back into the guy he knew so well.

Rigby had his Brennan back.

When he opened his eyes, his friend's eyes were open too. He saw his expression before Brennan looked hurriedly away.

"How long?" Rigby asked. "How long have you been in love with me?"

Brennan shook his head, he moved Rigby's hands off his face. "We don't have to talk about this."

"Yes, Bren, we do."

He just shook his head again and stepped back.

Rigby stayed with him, never letting more than three inches of air come between them.

"It's not your problem," Brennan told him.

"I'll decide what's my problem," Rigby said. "And you haven't answered my question."

"Don't you understand? Rig, you're only making it worse. Just forget it, please."

"Have you ever known me to back down?" Rigby demanded.

Brennan sighed.

"How long?" Rigby repeated. How long had he spent not noticing his best friend was hurting? And how many times had he told Brennan about his girlfriends, or thrown everything he did with them in Brennan's face without even realising everything he said made him flinch?

Brennan stalled for time, but they both knew he would answer eventually. "How the hell do you think I worked out I was gay in the first place?" he finally said. "It was you, Rig. It's always been you."

Rigby stared at Brennan's eyes, hoping his friend would look up, but Brennan kept his gaze firmly on the floor. He looked so scared and so alone, he looked so ready to run. Rigby couldn't let that happen. He wrapped his arms around Brennan, holding him close in to his chest.

Brennan tried to push him away. Rigby ignored that. "Hush," he whispered, folding him more securely into his arms.

"Rigby…"

"Shh…" he put his hand on the back of Brennan's head and coaxed his friend to tuck his face into his neck.

He reluctantly did as Rigby wanted for a few minutes. It didn't last. Brennan never did listen for very long. "I should…"

"Just let me think."

"There's nothing to think about," Brennan said. He tried to pull away again.

"Let me think," Rigby repeated.

With a long suffering sigh, Brennan gave up and rested his head against Rigby's shoulder, the way he'd wanted him to from the start. He felt good there. He felt right curled in close to Rigby's body.

Rigby's mind raced in the silence. Brennan was in love with him. The words circled through his mind again and again. Brennan, his Brennan, was in love with him. His Brennan. Rigby stroked his soft blond hair, soothing them both at the same time.

When Brennan tried to pull away a third time, Rigby just hushed him again. He had to think. He couldn't rush into anything this time. He'd rushed in blind with the kiss, but this was too important. He had to take a leaf out of Brennan's book and look before he leapt. He needed to think, because suddenly he didn't just have to make this minute okay, he had to make forever okay.

Rigby pressed a kiss onto Brennan's temple without even thinking about the gesture. Everything had to be made right for Brennan. Rigby closed his eyes. Brennan had to be happy. That was the most important thing. It was the only important thing.

When his friend started to fret again, Rigby rocked back and forth on his heels, hushing him gently with a soft noise in the back of his throat, the same sound he used to use when his little brother used to wake in the middle of the night from a bad dream, when Rigby was always the first one into his room to comfort him.

"We can't stand in the middle of the room forever," Brennan said.

It was a good point. He couldn't keep Brennan standing around. Rigby looked at his bed. Letting his friend out of his arms for the briefest possible moment, he took him by the wrist and led him across the room. Nudging Brennan onto the bed first he lay down on the outside of the mattress, coaxing Brennan to lie within the circle of his arms.

"Rig…"

"I can't work things out as quickly as you do, Bren. Just hush and let me think for a while."

"There's nothing to think about," Brennan protested.

Rigby stopped trying to convince him, he just held Brennan close, ignored all of Brennan's half hearted attempts to start a conversation.

Brennan was in love with him. He still couldn't wrap his mind around the concept. Best friends. When he was in the mood to risk sounding like a little girl, Rigby was willing to admit Brennan was his best friend forever. That was the way the world worked. Rigby closed his eyes and tried to let the idea they could ever be anything else settle into his mind.

He sighed. If Brennan was a girl everything would be so simple. He would slot so perfectly into Rigby's life. If he was honest with himself, Rigby knew deep down that most of his relationships with women ended when he measured the girl he was with against Brennan and found her severely wanting.

The only advantage girls had was sex. Rigby frowned. It wasn't so much of an advantage really... He thought back to the side of the pool, to Brennan's lips caressing his cock, to his fingers tightening in Brennan's hair. When it came to certain things, Rigby was pretty sure Brennan was the one with a clear advantage over all the girls in the world.

Perhaps he wasn't as straight as he thought he was—at least not with Brennan. Rigby stared at the wall behind Brennan's head. He could hardly accuse his friend of tricking him into being gay because he was effeminate, nor could he avoid liking all the things about Brennan which made him a man.

Maybe if he was with Brennan he'd have to get used to doing things a little bit differently than he did with girls, but he'd enjoyed oral sex and anal sex with women. There was no reason why those things shouldn't feel just as good with Brennan.

No, sex wasn't the stumbling block. That much had been made very obvious by the to do list.

Rigby held Brennan tighter. Picture after picture ran through his mind, showing him the way he expected his life to turn out. No matter how much he wanted to make things right for Brennan, he couldn't ignore the fact every single picture contained a woman standing at his side. He couldn't push away the idea that being bi enough to enjoy making out with his best friend didn't necessarily make him gay enough to spend the rest of his life with a man.

Rigby pressed a kiss to the top of Brennan's head. He closed his eyes and tried to think.

Chapter Five

Brennan tried not to enjoy the way Rigby's arms wrapped around him. If he let himself fall into the safe, warm feeling, it would only make it harder to accept the reality when his friend finally pushed him away. Brennan knew there was no other possibility. Rigby would have to push him away sooner or later.

"Rigby…"

When his friend tried to hush him again, Brennan shook his head. "No. My blurting everything out like that had to be a shock. I understand that you need time to think things through, but you don't need me to be here while you do that. Let me up."

Rigby shook his head.

"No," Brennan said with sudden determination. "In case you hadn't noticed—I didn't plan to say all that tonight. I never intended to have this conversation with you on any night. I need some time and space to think, too. So, let me up."

Rigby reluctantly responded to the plea in his voice and let him go. Brennan clambered over him. Space didn't help as much as he hoped it would. Standing in the middle of the room, Brennan didn't know where to go. He couldn't bring himself to grab his coat and leave, not without knowing what he had to come back to — if Rigby would be there for him to come back to at all. Brennan wavered back and forth in the middle of the room, trying to work out what to do now.

Damn he was stupid! Brennan kept asking himself over and over how the hell he could have said all that out loud. Rigby always wound him up. Brennan was the sensible one who listened to the shouting, waited until Rigby ran out of steam, and then calmly explained the way things were going to be.

He looked across at Rigby's worried expression.

"I'm so sorry," Rigby said softly.

No. That wasn't going to happen. "I don't want your pity," Brennan told him.

Rigby opened his mouth to speak.

Brennan turned around and looked out of the window. "And I don't need your pity either. I'm fine."

"You're in love with me."

There was no point denying it now. "Yes, but that's nothing new. I've been in love with you for years. I've dealt with it. You're straight. I'm not looking to convert you. I don't expect you to want anything more than friendship with me." He took a deep breath. It was the truth. Even after all the nonsense with the list, he never really believed he could be Rigby's first choice. "And if it's no longer possible for us to be friends then — "

"That's never been open to debate," Rigby said, anger at the idea lacing every word. "No matter what else happens, that doesn't change."

Brennan glanced over his shoulder. "Yes," he whispered, softly. Rigby had never given him cause to worry about their friendship. But all the panic he'd felt when he came out as gay swirled inside him again and he found it hard to believe anything was safe. "I don't want to lose that," he whispered.

"It's not going to happen," Rigby announced with all the confidence Brennan was so used to. It settled him a little to hear it. He could almost believe everything really was under Rigby's control.

He looked down over the grass quadrant opposite their building.

Rigby only stayed silent for a few seconds. "I wasn't apologising for now, I was apologising for before," he said.

Brennan frowned at the glass.

"If I'd known how you felt, the whole thing with the list would never have happened."

"Then I'm glad you didn't know," Brennan confessed. "I don't want to lie to you Rig, I enjoyed it—all of it. I won't wish it away. The only thing I'm sorry about is that you regret it now."

Rigby pushed a hand through his hair. Brennan pretended to look through the window while his gaze rested on Rigby's reflection in the glass.

"I enjoyed it too," Rigby admitted.

Brennan closed his eyes for a moment. Damn he hated doing the right thing. He hated telling the truth, especially when the truth truly sucked. "It doesn't mean anything."

Rigby looked up. "What?"

"You getting off on what we did together, it doesn't mean anything," Brennan said, each word sticking in his mouth.

"I'm pretty sure it means I'm not as straight as I always thought I was," Rigby said.

Brennan shook his head. "If a woman had a good technique and a reasonably understanding of male anatomy, she could probably get me off. It doesn't mean I'm straight, it doesn't mean I like women. It just means all guys are wired similarly enough—pushing the right buttons works on almost anyone."

Rigby shook his head. "It's not as simple as that."

"Only because you are making it complicated. You're straight. You indulged in a gay experiment. It's no big deal. The experiment's over. Now we just go back to the way things should be between us."

Rigby looked down at his hands.

Brennan glanced over his shoulder again. "This isn't something you need to fix, Rigby. I shouldn't have thrown how I felt at you that way. It's not your problem. It's just the way things are."

"It's just... I've always had these pictures in my head about the way my life is going to turn out," Rigby began.

"You don't have to explain," Brennan told him quickly. He really didn't need to hear that right now.

"Yes I do. I've always had these pictures—like little snap shots in my head. I'd get married and have kids and—"

"Rigby..." Brennan might have to live through all those things at some point, he might have to stand on the side lines and watch Rigby's life come together piece by white picket fence piece, but he didn't have to listen to it all—not right then. While Rigby was single, he might still keep Brennan around as a backup, but that would end the day he got married. Brennan knew he would never cheat on his wife.

"These fuzzy photos," Rigby repeated. "I didn't know who the girl would be or what the kids would look like or anything like that."

Brennan closed his eyes against the future.

"Everything was fuzzy," Rigby said again, "except one person. You were always there, Bren, in every single photo of my future, you're standing there right beside me, clear as anyone could ever be. If I take you out of the picture, I can't smile when I see it."

As Rigby looked up, Brennan met his eyes. "I'll still be there. I'm not going anywhere." He knew deep down that it was true. He would hang around for whatever scraps of Rigby's life he could be part of. If it meant being his backup screw, he'd just have to accept that. And if that meant being the best man at his wedding rather than the groom, he'd deal with that somehow, too.

Rigby shook his head. "You don't understand what I'm saying. Maybe the reason why I can't take you out of the picture is because you are the only one there who really matters to me."

"No."

Rigby blinked at him.

"No," Brennan repeated, just as firmly. "Stop trying to fix this. It won't work. Don't ask me to play pretend with you. I've seen gay men play at being straight and it always goes to hell. It won't work with a straight guy either."

Rigby looked down at his clasped hands as if the whole world played out along his white knuckles. "What about bi guys, does it work for them?"

Brennan shook his head. "You're not bi."

"I like having sex with men and women," Rigby said. "What else would you call me?"

Brennan sighed.

"You don't regret anything we've done?" Rigby checked after the silence between them stretched out for several minutes.

"No," Brennan admitted for the second time.

"Then we should keep going," Rigby declared.

Brennan closed his eyes against everything. When he opened them they went straight to the crumpled piece of paper on the far side of the room. That damn list... "No, we shouldn't." It wasn't until the words were out of his mouth that Brennan realised that they were true. He wasn't strong enough to deal with Rigby playing these sort of games with him.

"Why not? If what we've done so far hasn't hurt anything, then we should keep going," Rigby said again.

"You haven't thought this through," Brennan said. And although he wouldn't tell his friend that, it had already hurt him. Everything that made him believe he could have something real with Rigby hurt him because it made him hope for something he would never get.

"Yes, I have. I've been thinking this through since you said you love me, and it's going to work."

"Really? So tell me how it's going to work," Brennan demanded.

Rigby nodded to himself as if he really had all the answers. "We'll finish the list and then we stay together afterward."

Brennan shook his head. "You really think it's as simple as ticking things off a list?"

Rigby shrugged. "Why not?"

Brennan looked across at him. He wanted to take whatever he could get. It wasn't as if he couldn't enjoy bottoming for Rigby. But he couldn't let Rigby get any momentum into this insane idea that they would ever be more than friends once the list was done, he couldn't let himself believe such a dangerous idea. Brennan held back a sigh. "Because once around a list is completely different to having a relationship with someone."

"No, it's not," Rigby began.

"And because you don't even want the whole list, let alone more than that," Brennan cut in.

"Yes, I do," Rigby protested.

"So, bottoming was on your list as well as topping?"

Rigby hesitated.

Brennan refused to look down. "Once around the list for an experiment, you can pretend you're playing the 'man' and I'll put up with it. If you really wanted more than that, the rules would change." The rules would have to change for the sake of his own sanity. If he was going to be the second choice after a woman, he had to have something in his life to still tell him he was a man.

Rigby didn't look away, he didn't blink either.

Brennan smiled. Rigby never did think things through properly. He doubted his friend ever pictured him as a pitcher instead of a catcher. "I hate to break this to you, but if there weren't just as many gay men who topped as bottomed no one would have much fun."

"And you prefer to top?" Rigby realised.

"Yes." Brennan said, damned if he'd apologise for it right then.

Rigby looked him over as if he was actually thinking about it. Brennan wasn't insane enough to believe he really was.

Rigby might think it was his job to make his friend's life run smoothly — in between the times his schemes dropped him in trouble and his crazy ideas pulled him into some random insanity. Brennan was even half sure Rigby would top him to keep him happy or to fill the days when girls weren't available. But Brennan had no doubt bottoming would be a gay step too far for a guy like Rigby.

"All the time?"

Brennan blinked at his friend.

"Do you only top or do you bottom as well?" Rigby asked.

"Like I said, I'm versatile enough that I enjoy pretty much everything."

"For the record?" Rigby pushed.

Brennan's lips twitched up into a smile. "Yes, I enjoy bottoming too."

Rigby nodded. "So what's the problem? We'll... take it in turns or something," he said vaguely.

Brennan stared at his friend across the room and wondered the same thing. What was his problem? It wouldn't last, but it would be something. It would be something to remember while he lived through Rigby's picture album of perfect family moments.

While he watched Rigby fall for some girl and raise a family he could look back and remember the pleasure he saw in his lover's face, he could remember that for a little while, for whatever reason, Rigby wanted him.

Brennan knew he couldn't have what he truly wanted, but he had no idea why he should turn away the chance to enjoy what he could get. He looked at Rigby, he saw the determination in his eyes. Brennan could only say no to Rigby for so long.

He sighed. "This is a really stupid idea."

Rigby suddenly grinned, knowing he'd won for now.

He stood up. Brennan stayed frozen where he was. Rigby hooked a knuckle under his chin and tilted his head back the fraction needed to achieve the perfect angle. He brushed his lips against Brennan's as if he really wanted to kiss him.

Deepening the kiss, he slid his tongue into Brennan's mouth. He was so confident, so sure about everything. Brennan wished he felt the same. He tentatively took his hands out of his back pockets and put them on Rigby's waist, resting them against his belt.

Rigby tilted his head back further and pushed Brennan back until he was pinned to the wall. Brennan felt the window pane behind his head.

He nudged Rigby back.

Rigby frowned down at him. "What now?"

"Window."

Rigby looked from him to the glass and back again. "And?"

"Someone will see."

Rigby laughed. "You have sex in the back rooms of clubs and suddenly you're shy?"

"Someone will see you," Brennan explained as patiently as he could.

"And?"

"And I've put too much work into making sure no one thinks you are gay to have you throw it all away on a whim which might not even last out the night."

Rigby frowned down at him.

"Do really think the nearest gay bar is more than thirty miles away?" Brennan asked.

"What?"

"If everyone on campus knew you were sharing a room with a gay guy they'd assume you were gay too."

Rigby tucked his knuckle back under his chin and made him look up and meet his eyes. "You think you have to lie for me?"

Brennan shrugged. "Not everyone is like you, okay. A lot of people still have a problem with me. And they'd have a problem with you too if they knew you were friends with a gay man." They'd probably have a problem with a man who indulged in a gay experiment too, but Brennan wanted the experiment to continue too much to point that out right then.

"And what do you think would happen then?" Rigby demanded. "I'd walk away? I'd blame you? I'd take their side?"

Brennan shook his head and looked away. "No. You wouldn't do that. But these aren't school room bullies. It's not your job to make sure no one picks on me anymore."

"Someone hurt you."

Brennan wouldn't meet his eyes.

"Someone hurt you," Rigby repeated.

"Don't start on the stuck record thing again."

"Then tell me what happened," Rigby ordered.

"Nothing really. I've had a few run ins with people who didn't like my preferences, but nothing very serious — I'm far better at sarcasm than anyone who's ever tried to tell me I'm going to hell for preferring men. I just don't want you messed up in something which isn't your fight."

"Liar."

Brennan looked up at him but he couldn't hold Rigby's eye.

"You weren't mugged, were you? That black eye last summer," Rigby guessed.

Brennan sighed, realising Rigby was going to be as stubborn about this topic as he was about everything else. "I got beaten up coming out of a club."

"And you didn't even tell me?" Rigby demanded. "What happened?"

"They were waiting for some drunk to come out of the bar on his own." Brennan smiled slightly. "Only I wasn't drunk. And I remembered a few of those moves you taught me. I gave as good as I got."

"You should have told me," Rigby said. "I would have gone with you."

"To a gay bar?"

"Sure."

Brennan shook his head, trying not to remember how much he wanted to see Rigby walk into that club he'd got drunk in not so many days ago. "You might have cramped my style a bit," he said.

Rigby looked blank.

"I went there to get laid. Even if people didn't keep away thinking I was with you, most of them would probably have ended up hitting on you rather than me."

Rigby stroked his hair back from his face. "Don't sell yourself short. And yes, I would go with you if you were still going to places like that."

"I didn't stop going to gay bars, Rig. You don't let the bullies win—you taught me that."

Rigby smiled at the reminder of school days. "I meant you're not going looking for one night stands now we're together."

"So you don't just want a gay experiment, you actually want a monogamous gay experiment?" Brennan teased. He couldn't take it seriously because that would really mess up his head. It was far better to know Rigby was going to keep screwing women from the start.

"I want to see if we can make this work," Rigby said seriously. "And, yeah, that means I expect you to stop screwing around."

Brennan couldn't fight it any more. He just nodded. "Fine, if this is what you want. We'll try it. Nothing serious—just a good time until one of us wants to move on or you finish your to do list or whatever."

Rigby considered him for a long time. Brennan shifted uncomfortably under the intensity of his gaze. "If that's the best I can get from you at the moment, fine. But I'll give you advanced warning—I'm going to make sure you never want anyone else."

Brennan closed his eyes. As if there was any chance he would be the one who called Rigby's gay experiment off. When Rigby wanted to move on, he would step aside but he didn't have the strength to keep pushing Rigby away when he wanted nothing more than to wrap himself in Rigby and never let him go.

He opened his eyes. "You've got your work cut out then, because I've had some seriously good times with other guys. You've got some major competition."

Rigby grinned, he pushed Brennan up against the window again and took no notice when Brennan gave a half hearted protest against the very public location.

Tell wasn't working. That just left show as an option. Their lips moulded together. Rigby slid his tongue against Brennan's. Showing his friend he was serious was a lot more fun than talking about it.

If Brennan wanted to be shy, that was one thing. It was sweet in an inconsistently Brennan sort of way, but Rigby wouldn't let him be embarrassed about being together.

He walked them backwards and collapsed back on the bed, taking Brennan with him.

"Time to put your money where your mouth is," he murmured against Brennan's lips.

"You want to kiss my wallet?" Brennan asked between kisses. "And you said you weren't kinky…"

Rigby rolled Brennan onto his back. "Time to put your cock in my arse. Clear enough for you?"

Brennan gawped up at him as if he'd never heard those words before in his life.

Rigby cupped Brennan's growing erection through his jeans. "Tell me you're not up for it and I'll call you a liar."

Brennan shook his head. "No, it's okay, you can top."

"I know I can top. I'm very good at it. I fully intend to prove that to you at very frequent points in the future. But right now, you're going to top."

When Brennan tried to shake his head again, Rigby stilled him with his hand on the side of his face.

"You're not an experiment, Bren. I'm not just taking what I know I'll get off on. I'm serious about this."

Brennan seemed to freeze up. "If you're doing all this because you feel guilty about me falling for you, you can stop right now. Because, if you are offering me your arse as some sort of consolation prize..."

Rigby kissed him. It was a very convenient way to make Brennan stop talking when he stopped making any sense.

He grabbed Brennan's hand and pressed it against his crotch. "Does it feel like I'm not enthusiastic?"

Brennan hesitated, automatically stroking Rigby's cock through the fabric. One glance in his eyes and Rigby saw how much Brennan wanted this, and he saw the moment his friend stopped fighting it and just went with what Rigby wanted.

"The first time usually hurts," Brennan told him.

Rigby shrugged. "You survived. I'm sure I will too."

Brennan nodded.

Rigby studied his soon to be lover for any sign of his memories. "Who was he — your first time?"

"A guy in a bar," Brennan said.

"You don't even know his name?" Rigby demanded.

"Yes, I know his name. We introduced ourselves, hell we even shook hands before we got it on." Brennan saw Rigby's expression and seemed to change tack. "Look, he was a nice guy. We chatted a few times when I started going to the local bars. After a while we decided to have sex. He wasn't a nameless faceless stranger. He wasn't the love of my life either. I still see him around sometimes. We say hi. It wasn't some deep traumatic experience. It was just sex. I had a good time."

Rigby watched Brennan carefully. He didn't seem disturbed when he thought about the memories. The guy obviously hadn't been a complete bastard, that was something. "Is it okay if I still hate him?"

Brennan laughed. "I doubt it's going to be a big deal for him, since you don't know who he is and are unlikely to find out."

"Because you won't tell me?"

"Exactly," Brennan agreed.

Rigby set that aside to work on at a later date. He had more important issues right then. "I'm still bottoming tonight."

Brennan's hand slid from his crotch to rest on his backside, as if he couldn't quite resist the temptation. "Why?"

"Because I know I like topping," Rigby said simply. "If I like bottoming too, I think I've got this gay sex thing worked out pretty well."

"Some gay guys are exclusive tops—they don't like bottoming, so they don't. It's not a problem," Brennan offered.

"But you like topping."

Brennan nodded.

"So, you'll top."

Brennan stared at him for a while. Rigby watched him in return, trying to work out what he was thinking. A slow, amused smile spread across Brennan's face.

"What?" Rigby demanded.

"I always knew you'd be a pushy bottom," Brennan said.

"A what?"

"A bottom who acts like he's topping all the time."

Rigby considered the idea, sure he wasn't anything of the sort.

Brennan chuckled. "You're bossy and demanding and you always think you know what's best for everyone, especially me. When we have sex you'll be just the same."

"You've thought about having sex with me a lot," Rigby realised.

Against all of Rigby's expectations, a blush actually rose to Brennan's face.

"A real lot," Rigby guessed, smiling at the soft pink colour in his friend's cheeks.

"Yes."

"And what have you thought about?" Rigby whispered in his ear. "Have you been fantasising about my cock or my arse?"

Brennan closed his eyes. Rigby brushed his lips along Brennan's cheek and kissed his lips, teasing his mouth to respond.

"Your arse," he whispered against Rigby's lips.

"And yet you are still determined to argue with me about who is topping?"

Brennan leaned in for another kiss. "Damn, you are bossy," he muttered into the kiss.

Rigby smiled. "And I always get my own way in the end."

Brennan looked him up and down. "You know, it could be fun for you to give up control for a while."

Rigby chuckled. "Gay is still a work in progress—don't push your luck going for submissive too." He rolled Brennan onto his back and pinned him down.

Brennan rolled his eyes. "Yes, yes, very macho, very masculine. I'm very impressed and more than a little turned on. I'll be sure to remember this moment when I'm buried balls-deep in your arse."

Rigby grinned. Rolling them over, he pulled Brennan over with him and let his friend's weight settle on top of him. "Well, get on with it. You want to run the show, don't just stare at me like that."

Brennan pushed off him and retreated to his side of the room. "Your bed or mine?" Rigby asked, leaning on his elbow to watch Brennan look through his bedside drawer.

Brennan brought back a packet of condoms and a tube of lube, seemingly happy to use his friend's bed.

Condoms reminded him of something. "Do you always?" He asked, taking the packet, tossing it in the air and neatly catching it.

"Always for anal," Brennan said. "Usually for oral too—unless I know the guy really well and I'm sure he's clean." From his tone of voice Rigby guessed the latter didn't happen very often.

"I gave blood a few weeks ago," Rigby said. "I am clean."

"I know."

Rigby looked his query to Brennan.

"You wouldn't have let me go down on you if you weren't sure," Brennan said softly.

Rigby couldn't argue with his logic. He slid his hands under Brennan's shirt and ran them up his chest, pushing Brennan's shirt off over his head. He hadn't noticed just how well defined Brennan's body was until he got up close and personal with it. He ran his fingers over the hard lines of muscle, enjoying the way they felt under his fingers.

A moment later Rigby's shirt was gone too. He reached for his friend's jeans. Brennan reached for his. Their hands slid past each other as if they'd been undressing each other for years. As if it was the most natural thing in the world.

Lips trailing kiss after kiss against each other's mouths, they lay back down on Rigby's bed.

"Roll over."

Rigby blinked at him.

"It's more comfortable for you if I'm behind you, especially the first time," Brennan explained. When Rigby wanted to speak, Brennan covered his lips with his hand. "If you ask me if it's what I want then I might hit you over the head with something very heavy."

Rigby moved Brennan's hand out of the away. "And what's wrong with me asking you about your favourite position?"

"Nothing. But you're fast convincing me that this is a onetime shot to make me feel better. It feels like, as soon as we zip up, you're going to walk out of this room and I'm never going to set eyes on you again."

Brennan sounded so worried about that prospect, Rigby didn't argue. He rolled over. Brennan lightly stroked his back as if he thought he needed gentling down. It felt good, so Rigby let it go on for a few minutes before he got bored.

"Yes, I know. Hurry up," Brennan said. Rigby heard the smile in his voice. Brennan slid a hand down over his buttocks and slipped his hand between his legs.

His first instinct was to pull the hell away from some guy stroking between his cheeks. He didn't hide the automatic flinch quickly enough. Brennan's other hand stroked his back again.

"The whole go slow thing is frustrating as hell," Rigby complained.

"Shut up."

Rigby smiled until Brennan's hand disappeared altogether. "What…"

"Hush."

Brennan's fingers slid against him again, slick with something. His mind supplied the necessary guess work. Lube. He turned a little further onto his stomach and gave Brennan better access between his legs.

"It feels strange at first," Brennan said softly. "You just need to relax and go with it."

Brennan's finger slid inside him. Rigby clamped down around it, not sure if he wanted to push it away or hold it inside him forever. Brennan was right. It was a strange sensation. Brennan stayed still inside him for a few seconds then began to move.

"Are you going to get going now?" Rigby demanded.

"Patience."

"It doesn't hurt."

Brennan chuckled. "That's great. Now all you have to do is find a guy with a cock the same size as my finger and you really are good to go."

Rigby shot Brennan a dirty look over his shoulder.

Brennan smiled back at him. "When you can take three fingers without squirming, you're ready to have some real fun."

Rigby rolled his eyes. "And you have the nerve to call me bossy."

"I know what I'm doing, and you don't. This is probably the only chance I have to top without receiving helpful hints on how to do it better. I'm just making the most of it," Brennan said.

"I know what I'm doing. I've topped women for anal — she didn't need this amount of prep."

"And she probably even convinced you anal was your idea," Brennan muttered.

"It was."

"She probably did the prep before you even got there."

Rigby glared at him over his shoulder. He thought through a few alternative answers, before he settled on the most suitable one. "Don't pick on the straight guy. I was at a statistical disadvantage in understanding my previous lovers. Women are not designed to be understood."

Brennan's finger slid further inside him and made a weird crooking motion. Rigby wondered what the hell he was doing. Then he almost jumped off the bed.

"Prostate," Brennan whispered in his ear.

"I know what it is," Rigby said. "I just never realised it was so…" He pushed back against Brennan's finger, trying to press it against his prostate again.

Brennan chuckled in his ear. "Just like this." He moved his finger again, pressed against that perfect little spot.

Rigby moaned his appreciation.

"Ready for more?" Brennan asked.

"I was ready for more ten minutes ago," Rigby reminded him. "You're the one who thinks I'm made of glass."

Brennan took his finger away and slid two back in its place. Rigby could really feel the stretch at that. He still pushed back against Brennan's fingers demanding more. "Three."

Brennan obviously wasn't finding the waiting easy either. He only made Rigby wait a few more frustrating minutes before he slid a third finger in with the other two.

Ouch! Rigby bit his lip and pushed back anyway.

Brennan's fingers stilled inside him. "It's not a competition in bloody mindedness, Rig. Take your time now and it will feel better when it's my cock inside you. And I want it to feel good for you."

Rigby fell still trying to work out the right move.

"Let me make it good for you?" Brennan asked.

Rigby twisted his spine so he so he could look over his shoulder and into Brennan's eyes. He looked so damn serious.

"It feels damn good now."

Brennan touched his cheek with his left hand while the other's fingers rested idly inside him. Brennan leaned over and kissed him on the lips. "You're really sure about this?" he murmured.

"Yes." Rigby was sure he was very sure.

Brennan grabbed the condoms from the bedside table and quickly sheathed himself in the thin latex. A moment later he lined up against Rigby's back. It wasn't the same as fingers. The blunt pressure didn't coax its way inside him like Brennan's fingers. Rigby pushed back against Brennan's cock as Brennan slid slowly inside him, filling him more than Rigby believed was physically possible.

Brennan fell still behind Rigby. "Perfect," he whispered.

Rigby just nodded and tried to remember how to breathe.

"That's right," Brennan whispered. "Just try and relax around me, it will get easier."

He stayed still inside Rigby for an impossibly long time as the burning stretch settled into a pleasant ache. Then he started to move. Brennan really did know what he was doing. A woman never had Rigby biting his lip to keep from moaning their name.

Sure he should be making a more active contribution to proceedings, Rigby reached behind him and blindly tried to grab Brennan and demand a faster rhythm.

Brennan's hand covered his and politely moved it out of his away. "Just take it," he coaxed in a soft, breathless whimper. "Please? You can be bossy next time. This time just let go and enjoy it. Let me make this good for you?"

Rigby bit back another whimper as he did his best to do as his lover asked.

Brennan thrust harder into him and reached around him to wrap his hand around his cock. Rigby couldn't hold back the weak little noise in the back of his throat. Brennan's hand and his cock worked in counterpoint, each burst of pleasure racing along his nerve endings was followed by another until Rigby couldn't tell if the pleasure was coming from his cock or his prostate, he just knew it was more pleasure than he'd ever believed existed in the world.

Far sooner than he wanted, Rigby jerked and spilled his cum over the blanket and Brennan's hand. Brennan kept moving inside him, pounding pleasure into Rigby's body until he finished himself off with a series of harsh thrusts that pushed Rigby towards the wall. He clumsily put a hand out and braced himself against the plaster work, giving Brennan a more stable target as he approached and fell into his climax.

Brennan stilled and rested his head on Rigby's shoulder. Rigby stayed frozen where he was too. Finally, Brennan moved, gently pulling out and turning away to dispense with his condom.

Rigby rolled away from the sticky patch he'd created on his bed sheet. "Now I know why you picked my bed rather than yours," he grumbled.

Brennan grinned. He looked amazingly happy with the world. In the midst of afterglow, he was truly stunning. Rigby stood up. He picked Brennan up and dropped him back down on Brennan's neatly made bed. Tugging at the sheets, Rigby pulled the blanket up over Brennan and he slid in next to him.

"Yeah, sure, I don't mind sharing," Brennan muttered.

It was hard to take his protest seriously when he cuddled into Rigby's embrace with only the mildest coaxing. "We'll have to get a place with a double bed," Rigby realised.

Brennan tensed in his arms. "I'm not sure that's a good idea."

"I like double beds. I like room to move around when screwing," Rigby informed him. He could just imagine Brennan stretched out for him on a double bed, he could just imagine all the things he could do with his friend in that situation.

Brennan curled closer even as he shook his head. "Just leave things as they are for now."

"You mean until I go back to being straight?" Rigby asked.

Brennan shrugged.

"I don't think that would have felt half as good if you'd had to wear a strap on."

"Rig…" Brennan protested.

"Bren, I wouldn't play games with this—not with you. This is what I really want."

Brennan turned his face more into his shoulder and pretended to fall asleep. Rigby held his lover closer and let him pretend for a while.

Chapter Six

It wasn't going to last, but Brennan could still enjoy it while it did. He kept his eyes closed as he snuggled closer to Rigby's sleeping form.

"Stop wriggling."

Rigby's not so sleeping form...

For a few moments, Brennan let himself pretend he would wake up that way every day. Then he forced himself to open his eyes and face reality.

He glanced up. Rigby was half sitting up, pillows folded behind his back while Brennan rested comfortably against his sloping chest. He had a note book balanced on his lap. "What are you doing?" Brennan asked, wiping the sleep out of his eyes.

Rigby frowned and tapped his pen against the note book. "Making a new list."

Brennan craned his neck and tried to see what Rigby had written. He only caught sight of the word *Her.* "Oh," Brennan pulled away from his friend. Ticking off the gay list obviously only turned out to be fun for one of them. He knew he should have insisted on bottoming. It was too late for that now.

"Where are you going?"

"Bathroom," Brennan muttered.

Rigby let him past. Brennan grabbed his towel and wrapped it around his waist, tucking his wash bag under his arm on the way out of their room.

He couldn't meet his own gaze in the mirror above the sink as he cleaned his teeth. It was his own fault for falling in with Rigby's stupid ideas so easily. When he heard the door leading into the communal bathroom open, he quickly hung up his towel and slipped into one of the shower stalls. He wasn't ready to face the rest of the world yet, not while he still felt like the word idiot was stamped on his forehead.

It was Rigby. Brennan always knew when it was Rigby walking into a room. He shook his head at himself and ducked his head under the spray as he adjusted the flow and raised the temperature slightly.

He listened to Rigby banging about on the other side of the curtain. Eyes closed, he couldn't help but imagine it wasn't a university hall of residence. He couldn't help but wonder what it would be like to share a similar morning routine with Rigby in a house they lived in together after they graduated.

Stupid! He should never have let Rigby talk him into any of this. It just made it harder to remember what the reality really was. The shower curtain moved. Rigby calmly nudged him further into the stall to make room for him.

"What the hell are you doing?" Brennan hissed at him.

Rigby pushed him back against the wall and kissed him.

Brennan tried to protest, but the sound was lost against Rigby's mouth. When he tried to push Rigby away, Rigby just caught his wrists and pinned them to the tiles.

"Have you lost your mind?" Brennan demanded the moment Rigby left his lips.

"Good morning to you too," Rigby said with a smile.

Brennan glared at him.

Rigby just chuckled. "You look good wet," he observed. "I meant to say that at the pool, but the blowjob pushed it out of my mind."

Brennan kept his gaze fixed firmly on Rigby's face. He was not going to check Rigby's body out. He was not going to return the compliment. He was not going to acknowledge being pinned to the wall was making him harder by the moment.

Rigby leaned against him and rocked his hips, making sure Brennan knew he was entirely aware of his problem. His friend was also hard. Brennan swallowed as his own arousal went up another notch. "How's your list going?" he asked.

"Great." Rigby kissed his neck. "Shall I tell you all the things I want to do with you?"

"With me?"

Rigby pulled back so he could look down at him, but he still wouldn't let go of Brennan's wrists. "Who else?"

"The list said her," Brennan reminded him.

Rigby frowned. "I know my hand writing sucks, but I'm damn sure I know what gender I was writing about screwing."

"I saw it on the list, Rig." Brennan tried to pull his hands out of Rigby's grip again. "I meant what I said, no harm no foul. We can just forget about all this and go back to being friends."

"Pity I'm not as forgiving as you then, because I'm not just going to nod and smile if you call this off now."

Brennan looked up at Rigby, he looked genuinely pissed off. Brennan closed his eyes and rested his head back against the tiles. His head swirled with ideas shooting off in all different directions. "I don't know if I can do this," he whispered.

"Bren?" Rigby's tone immediately altered. He let go of Brennan's wrists to pull him into his arms. He wouldn't let Brennan put any space between them. "Hey, you know it doesn't really matter what's on the list, you know that nothing you don't want will ever happen between us, right? You know I'd never hurt you."

Brennan rested his head on Rigby's shoulder. As much as he wanted to deny it, Rigby holding him close felt as good as he always imagined it would. But Brennan also knew Rigby was the only guy he'd ever screwed who really could hurt him. He didn't mind a few whips and chains, but Rigby leaving him scared the hell out of him. When there was no possibility that Rigby would stick around forever, that left Brennan no option but to live scared and he didn't know if he could cope with that.

Rigby kissed the top of his head. "Everything's going to be fine. You'll see, Bren. I'm going to look after you now."

"I don't need looking after," Brennan said firmly, pushing away the idea Rigby would want to look after him in the long term. "I'm not a girl, Rigby, don't treat me like one." He put enough distance between them to look up at Rigby and look him in the eye.

Rigby smiled down at him.

"What?"

"What's need got to do with it. I like looking after you."

Brennan looked down. The words were spoken with such calm certainty, it was hard to see anything but the dominance behind them. Brennan swallowed. No. He couldn't let himself see meanings in Rigby's words that weren't there. Rigby never thought things through, that had to lead to a lot of words that didn't mean anything.

Rigby stroked his fingers through Brennan's hair and kissed his temple. "Everything will be fine."

Brennan nodded.

Rigby turned off the shower and grabbed the towel. He dried Brennan off himself, refusing to give up control of Brennan's towel until he wrapped it around Brennan's waist and took his own off the hook outside the shower stall.

Brennan walked across the room and leaned against the sink. "Joining me in the shower was a really stupid idea. Anyone could have walked in."

"Yeah," Rigby agreed cheerfully. "I enjoyed it too. We'll have to share more often."

Brennan shook his head and watched Rigby dry himself off. On the way down the hall, Rigby slung his arm around Brennan's shoulders. Brennan slipped out of his loose hold and went straight into their room.

As soon as the bedroom door closed behind them, Rigby tumbled them both onto the bed. He offered Brennan the pen and the note book he'd been writing on. "Feel free to cross out or add on whatever rocks your boat."

Rigby sprawled along the outside edge of the bed. Brennan had hardly any room. He either had to be pressed up tight against the wall or against Rigby's body. He tried a nudge or two to see if that would gain him any mattress, but Rigby was as solid as a boulder when he wanted to stay put. Brennan sighed and turned his attention to the list.

He scanned down. It seemed like a pretty thorough list of things to do. From a better angle, he also saw the word *her* transform into he with a randomly added squiggle testifying to Rigby's poor penmanship.

"Handcuffs?" Brennan asked as he reached the middle.

"Does the idea freak you out?" Rigby asked.

He sounded so concerned, it was all Brennan could do not to laugh out loud. "I think I could cope with handcuffs," he said carefully.

"Great. We'll have to go shopping for some later," Rigby said.

Brennan glanced at his bedside drawer. Some bits of information were probably best left for a different day and there was no telling when an extra pair of cuffs could come in handy. He nodded. "Shopping," he agreed, in a tone of voice he hoped would indicate he'd never even seen a pair of handcuffs in his life, let alone got hard picturing him and Rigby having considerable fun with a pair.

* * * *

Between their different lectures, they didn't make it to a sex shop to buy the handcuffs that day. Brennan couldn't really regret that. As much as he was looking forward to any sort of bondage making an appearance in their future, there was something very enjoyable about shared glances as they passed each other on the way to different lecture halls.

There was something even better about ducking into shadowy corners and stealing kisses from each other. Lips against lips, hushed murmurs and bitten back laughter while people walked past feet away all made Brennan lightheaded with pleasure. After the first three times, Brennan couldn't even pretend to be pissed off with Rigby for being so indiscreet.

Brennan looked across the students' union to where Rigby was taking two bottles of beer from a bartender. Rigby grinned as he made his way back to him and handed him a bottle. For once in Brennan's life it felt safe not to worry about Rigby finding a girl and disappearing half way through the night.

Rigby had made it quite clear a few more things would be ticked off his list that night.

"Pool?" Rigby asked, nodding to where two girls were leaving the table.

Brennan nodded agreeably. He was perfectly sure he would agree to anything Rigby suggested that night.

"Ever done it on a pool table?" Rigby whispered in his ear as he handed him a cue.

Brennan choked on his beer. He shot an unimpressed glare at his friend, who laughed and tossed back his own beer without so much as a hiccup.

"You, know, Tammy works as a barmaid here."

Brennan hesitated as he lined up for the break. "As in one of your ex-girlfriends has a key to somewhere where you want to have sex," he translated, his mind flashing back to the side of the pool. From there it was easy to skip forward to the kiss — to Rigby kissing him not because there was something he wanted to tick off a list, but just because he wanted to.

Rigby grinned.

Brennan completely trashed his shot. Since he was picturing Rigby bent over the table rather than the cue ball, he wasn't entirely surprised.

"Tonight?" Brennan asked.

Rigby took his shot. Sank one of the yellow balls and smiled his satisfaction. "No, not tonight. I feel like doing something different tonight."

Brennan nodded his understanding. He waited for Rigby to take another shot. Then he waited for Rigby to tell him just what he had in mind. Rigby just smiled to himself. He'd been hinting without providing any details all day and he obviously had no intention of telling his friend then. Brennan let the subject drop. It was just too much fun to spend the evening imagining possibilities to push the issue.

Rigby won the pool game. Brennan smiled at him across the table, unable to care who won when he was enjoying the game so much. Rigby smiled back for a moment, then he seemed to lose focus and look past him.

Brennan looked over his shoulder, but he couldn't spot anyone they both knew in the crowd. By the time he looked back around to his friend Rigby had set his pool cue to one side.

"There's something I need to do," he said on the way past.

Brennan nodded. He smiled to himself because he knew Rigby would be back. It was a fantastic feeling. Brennan hung around the pool table talking to a few of the guys he knew from his physics lectures but after a while he started to look at his watch and wonder where Rigby had disappeared to.

When he bumped into one of the other men from their halls of residence, he gave into the temptation to ask. "You seen Rigby anywhere?"

"He's screwing some blonde out by the gents," he said.

Brennan tried not to show any reaction. Rigby had a well deserved reputation for screwing around. Their friend was just guessing. Rigby wasn't really screwing anyone, he wouldn't screw someone else tonight of all nights.

He stared at the pool table for a while, not really seeing the game. Rigby probably wouldn't want to wait around once he decided to leave the bar, Brennan decided to take a visit to the gents' room, just to take a leak, so he would be ready to leave when Rigby showed up again.

Brennan stopped at the end of the dark passageway, leading to the toilets. Rigby stood down the far end of it with a blonde. As Brennan watched, she giggled and pushed her body against his. Rigby's hand slid further around her waist and pulled her closer into his arms.

Yeah, Brennan thought to himself, Rigby felt like doing something different that night, he wanted to do someone different too. Brennan stood there for what felt like hours, watching Rigby and the woman he'd obviously selected to be his first choice that night. When Rigby turned and looked in Brennan's general direction, Brennan stepped back around the corner.

He couldn't let Rigby see him watching. He had to get out of there. Brennan bounced from drunken student to drunken student until he tumbled out of the students' union. Even outside he couldn't get a proper lung full of air. He leaned against the brick wall and closed his eyes very tight, trying not to hyperventilate. Rigby still hadn't stopped going on about the last time after all these years. He'd never let him live it down if it happened again.

Brennan banged his head back against the wall as he straightened up. It failed to knock any sense into him.

"You okay?"

For a moment, Brennan thought those words belonged to Rigby, he thought Rigby might have come out of the club after him. He actually thought there might be some logical explanation for the blonde.

The man standing a few feet away looked familiar, but he wasn't Rigby.

"I'm fine, thanks," Brennan said automatically and transferred his gaze back to the floor.

"Still having problems with the straight hand job guy?" the man asked.

Brennan jerked his gaze back to the man.

"Oh, God, I'm sorry. You were in the bar in Cardiff. I thought you were out," his voice dropped into a whisper as he said it.

Brennan shrugged. "I am out, sort of, I mean..." He banged his head back against the bricks again. "I'm an idiot."

The guy didn't seem entirely sure what to say to that.

Brennan studied him a little more closely. "You're the bartender," he realised. "Um… if I was any trouble after I got drunk," he began.

The bartender brushed that aside. "You weren't any trouble, you just seemed…" he trailed off, coming closer to lean on the wall next to him.

Brennan gave a sad laugh. "I think the word you're looking for is pathetic. It's just that he's…" Brennan didn't even know what to say about Rigby. "He's just, him, you know?"

The guy nodded like he knew what Brennan was talking about.

"He's having sex with a blonde by the gents' toilets," Brennan blurted out.

"Ouch! And, while he's doing that, you are?"

Brennan shook his head at himself. "I'm trying to convince myself that it would be really stupid to stick around here now. But I pretty sure I'm actually going to stay right here until he comes out of the bar. And I'm going to spend all the time he's in there screwing her, hoping he'll still want a blow job off me when we go back to our room."

The guy stood up. "Come on."

"What?"

"There's a gay bar just around the block from here, I'll buy you a drink."

Brennan shook his head. "I'm not out at the university."

"Why not?"

"Because I'm sharing a room with a straight guy and…"

"And because you run your whole life according to what makes his life easier?"

Brennan shrugged.

"Look, my name's Mike. I'm not a weird straight guy, so I doubt I'm your type, but I'm a good listener, and I think that's what you could use right now."

Brennan looked back to the students' union.

If he waited here Rigby might...

He looked up and saw the sympathy shining in Mike's eyes. He wasn't Rigby, but maybe that was what Brennan needed right then, someone who wasn't Rigby. And it wasn't like Rigby would finish with the girl any time soon. If he wanted that blow job it wouldn't be until much later in the evening.

Brennan took a deep breath. "Where exactly is that bar?"

* * * *

Rigby disentangled himself as politely impossible from Lucy's clinging touch. He led her back to a table full of her friends and made his excuses. Then he went to look for Brennan. Ten minutes later he was half ready to believe his friend had disappeared off the face of the planet.

He'd left him by the pool table. Brennan should still be there when Rigby went back to him. That was the way the world worked. It wasn't like Brennan to wander off on his own when they went out together.

"I didn't know your roommate was gay."

Rigby turned around and came face to face with a guy from his halls of residence. "What?"

"You're rooming with Brennan Talbot, right?"

Rigby nodded.

"Adam just saw him going into the gay bar on Johnson Street."

Rigby frowned. "Are you sure?"

"Adam's in all his physics classes, he should know Brennan when he sees him. You really didn't know he's gay?"

Rigby didn't stick around to answer. He was out of the students' union and half way down Johnson Street before he even thought about what he was doing.

The bouncer stopped him at the door.

"Damn it, Carl, you know I'm over eighteen. I'm in your classics tutorial." Rigby shrugged the guy's hand off his arm and tried to step past him.

Carl still blocked his way. "You never mentioned in any of those classes that you were gay," he observed.

"I'm not gay," Rigby said.

For some reason Carl still wouldn't let him into the bar. "This is a gay bar."

"I know," Rigby said.

"And you're straight," Carl pointed out, as if they hadn't already covered that point.

"Yeah, well my boyfriend's gay, so if you'll get out of my way," Rigby hinted.

"You're straight and you have a gay boyfriend," Carl asked.

Rigby just glared at him. What he and Brennan were to each other was no one else's business. He should probably speak to Brennan about them both being out before he made any further declarations on the point.

Carl finally gave up and let him into the club, with a shrug of his shoulders and a muttered comment about closet cases.

Brennan had obviously had a change of heart about being out around the university. He stood right there in plain sight, next to the bar with several men.

"Are you drunk?" one of them asked Brennan, as Rigby came into earshot of them.

"No," Brennan said. As far as Rigby could tell, he sounded sober enough for it to be the truth.

"I'm just asking, because it's a hell of a jump from being in the closet to being the only catcher in a five-some."

That conversation had certainly gone far enough. Rigby marched straight into the middle of the group. He grabbed hold of Brennan's wrist and pulled him aside.

"What the hell?" one of the guys asked.

While Rigby was distracted by him, Brennan tried to shake him off and pull his arm away. That wasn't going to happen.

"I don't know what the hell you were thinking coming here-" Rigby began, turning his complete attention to Brennan.

"Please don't do this, Rigby." He made it sound like Rigby was doing something wrong. Like there was nothing wrong with Brennan going to a gay bar on his own when they were supposed to be together. "Just leave me be," Brennan pleaded.

Rigby stared at his friend. Brennan looked so sad, and Rigby had no idea how to fix that look this time.

"I can't do it, okay?" Brennan said. "I can't just watch you go off to Alice or the blonde or – "

"Who's Alice?" Rigby cut in.

"The girl who bailed on you the night I got drunk," Brennan reminded him.

Rigby looked blankly at his friend. "The night you got drunk I didn't have a date that night, I had a late lecture."

"Please don't lie," Brennan said. "That just makes it worse."

"I had a lecture on Alice Walker," Rigby said very slowly, in the vain hope it might help Brennan understand.

"No, you didn't."

"Um…" One of the guys who'd been talking to Brennan when he came in, put his hand up for permission to interrupt. Rigby glared at him. "He did have a lecture, I was there. Alice Walker, The social and ethical questions raised and discussed in *The Color Purple*."

Brennan looked at the guy for a moment, as if analysing if he could believe him, then he turned back to Rigby. "And who were you studying when you were screwing the blonde by the gents' toilet tonight?" he asked.

"Lucy?" Rigby tried to keep up. "I'm not screwing Lucy."

"I saw you all wrapped around her, Rig. I'm not stupid."

"Five minutes ago I thought you were one of the smartest men I've ever met," Rigby told him. "But if you think I would go off and screw someone else while I was on a date with you, you really don't have a clue."

"You're straight," Brennan began.

"If you still won't believe I'm bi after last night, stupid doesn't come close," Rigby snapped. They stared at each other.

"Brennan," the guy on Rigby's left began to say.

Brennan was his and Rigby didn't want anyone else even talking to Brennan right then. The guy put his hand on Brennan's shoulder, as if he was the person who looked after Brennan, as if he was the one who had the right to touch Brennan any time he chose.

Rigby tugged Brennan away from the other man. His friend over balanced and topped towards Rigby. He landed perfectly in his arms. Rigby nodded to himself, very pleased with that result.

Chapter Seven

Brennan looked up at his friend, trying to work out what was going on. "Rigby?" he asked.

Rigby offered him a half smile. He stroked his cheek. "It's going to be okay," he said.

Brennan shook his head. "No, it's not. I can't do this, Rig," he whispered.

"Can't do what, Bren?" Rigby asked.

"I can't crawl around for scraps, Rig, it messes with my head. I know I said I'd stick around for whatever I could get, but I can't. I could deal with not being on your radar. I could take knowing you would never see me as anything more than a friend, but I can't cope with living my whole life hoping your first choice bails so I can get laid. I just can't."

"Bren," Rigby tried to say.

Brennan just shook his head again. "I'll put in for a transfer to a new room tomorrow and..." he bit his lip, trying desperately to keep his emotions in check.

"Room 39."

Brennan blinked up at his friend. "I don't understand."

"A guy on one of my classics courses broke up with his girlfriend, he's looking to move from a double room to a twin. I saw him in the bar. I told him we wanted to swap rooms with him. I told you last night that I wanted us to get a room with a big double bed, remember?"

Brennan looked down. "And what, Lucy was just a way to pass your time on the way back to me?" he asked, as if he was daring Rigby to agree with him.

"Lucy's a sweet girl, we had some fun together a few months back. I crashed into her on my way out of the gents' and I wasn't about to leave her on her on her own in the bar when she was completely out of her head. But all I did was keep her on her feet and listen to some convoluted story about her roommate until I could find her friends. You're the one who wandered off to find a cheap screw the moment I turned my back."

Brennan shook his head. "It wasn't like that, I..." He closed his eyes and just tried to think. He'd had it all worked out when Rigby wasn't there. He had a whole speech ready, how he was going to explain to his friend that this nonsense with the list couldn't go on. It all went out of his head now Rigby was there.

"If this is going to work between us, you can't run off to a gay bar every time I look at a woman," Rigby whispered to him, pulling him closer. "You have to have a bit more faith in me."

Brennan rested his forehead on Rigby's shoulder, but that was more from exhaustion than anything else. He was just so tired of not knowing what was going on in his life, of not even knowing what was going on inside his own head.

"I screw around when I'm single, but I don't cheat on someone I'm dating, Bren. You should know me better than that."

"We're not dating," Brennan said. "We're doing the list and then, if you want to repeat anything on the list we might... we might do that but..."

Rigby hushed him.

Brennan just wanted to close his eyes and be held close. He was so tired of it all. He didn't want to think about anything else, he just wanted to pretend for a while. He wanted to pretend his mind wasn't falling apart and Rigby really meant everything he said.

"Come on," Rigby said, "I'm taking you back to our room."

He couldn't walk away from Rigby twice in one night. He knew he'd only managed it once because Rigby wasn't actually there at the time. Brennan gave up. Brennan let Rigby lead him out of the bar.

* * * *

In their room, Brennan couldn't even raise a sarcastic comment. He decided he'd just let what was going to happen, happen regardless. Maybe one day he'd be able to say no to whatever he could get from Rigby, but today wasn't that day. Rigby led him over to his bed. Brennan stared blankly at it until Rigby nudged him to sit on the mattress.

Rigby crouched down in front of him and looked him in his eye.

"What's going on in that head?" Rigby asked, stroking the hair at his temple.

"I..." Brennan closed his eyes. "I didn't mean for you to follow me into the bar," he said. He hadn't meant to out his friend as well as everything else. "If I put in for a new room tomorrow, everyone will just assume that you didn't want to share with me once you found out I'm gay and..."

"My biggest problem isn't that I'm out as being bi," Rigby said firmly. "I'm sure I'll get used to that quickly enough. My biggest problem is that I have no idea what went wrong between us. A few days ago I'd swear you'd trust me with your life. Now I can't step out of your sight without you thinking that I'm cheating on you. I have no idea how that happened."

Brennan shook his head. "I do trust you," he said quietly.

"You have a funny way of showing it, Bren." Rigby said the words softly, but Brennan could tell he was hurt by the accusation.

Brennan's mind went back to Lucy hanging all over Rigby in the corridor. Fear poured back into him, but with Rigby right there in front of him, he realised what he was actually afraid of.

Seeing the hurt in Rigby's eyes, he had no choice but to confess the truth. "I'd let you," he admitted.

"What?"

Brennan closed his eyes. "I'm not scared you'd screw around, I'm scared I'd let you," he whispered. "Do you have any idea what that feels like, Rig? Knowing I'd just stand there and accept whatever you do, because I'd rather be your second choice or your

Kim Dare

third choice or your anything at all as long as I can be something to you?"

Rigby sat up on the bed next to him and pulled Brennan into his arms. He held him so tight, Brennan could hardly breathe. He buried his face in Rigby's shoulder, desperate to be as close to him as he could possibly be.

"Hush, it's okay, I've got you," Rigby whispered in his ear. "It's okay."

"It's not okay," Brennan told him. "I'm supposed to be quick and sarcastic and I can't be this way — I can't be this pathetic."

"You're not pathetic," Rigby told him.

"Don't you get it? I am, I…"

"No!" There was real snap to Rigby's voice. "I don't want to hear you talking about yourself like that."

Brennan shrugged.

"You don't have to worry about what you'd let me do, Bren. I wouldn't let myself hurt you like that."

Brennan looked down.

Rigby made him look up at him. "You think it only goes one way. Do you really think I would have raced off after anyone else if they walked away in the middle of a date with me? You weren't the only one who couldn't turn his back on his boyfriend when he thought he was screwing around."

Brennan saw the truth in Rigby's eyes. He looked away. "I've really screwed all this up, haven't I?"

"Did you have sex with any of them before I got there?" Rigby asked.

Brennan shook his head.

"You can tell me the truth," Rigby whispered in his ear. "It's okay, I won't be mad."

211

In spite of everything, Brennan smiled at that. "Liar."

Rigby half chuckled himself. "Yeah, I think I might have found a jealous side I never knew I had," he acknowledged. "But tell me anyway?"

"I didn't do anything," Brennan told him seriously.

"So, we're both okay," Rigby decided.

They were quiet for a while, just sitting there huddled close to each other, neither of them prepared to break the moment of tentative understanding by moving first.

Brennan considered his options. If Rigby hadn't actually screwed around behind his back, it wasn't too pathetic to ask. He could ask his... his possible boyfriend if he was in the mood. "Do you want to tick something off your list?"

Rigby smiled down at him. "If we'd made it to the shop I'd vote for the handcuffs idea. You have no idea how much I'd love to see you in cuffs right now."

Brennan considered his options. He wanted the same thing. He wanted it so much it felt more like a primal need than anything he had any control over. "Second drawer down," he blurted out.

"What?"

Brennan looked at his bed side cabinet.

Rigby frowned and opened the drawer. He extracted a pair of handcuffs. "You went to the shop?"

Brennan shook his head.

Rigby looked at the cuffs for a long time. "You're into this then?" he asked, looking back at the other items in the drawer.

"I've dabbled with it," Brennan said carefully.

"You let random guys you met in a club tie you up?" Rigby demanded, obviously appalled at the idea.

Brennan shook his head. "I wasn't usually the guy wearing the cuffs in the clubs."

Rigby frowned at them. "So you don't like wearing them yourself."

Brennan shrugged. "Not with random guys in clubs — I do have some sort of survival instinct."

"With me?" Rigby asked.

Brennan couldn't meet Rigby's eye. He shrugged and pretended he didn't care. "I guess I can trust you not to turn into a psychopath half way through the scene," he said.

He glanced at the handcuffs in Rigby's hands. His friend appeared fascinated by them. Rigby reached out and took hold of Brennan's wrist. He traced the line where the cuffs would lie with his finger tips. "Now." It was a statement, not a question.

Brennan wanted to feel like he belonged to Rigby so much he couldn't even think of a sarcastic response to the demand. He just nodded.

In seconds all their clothes were tossed aside. Rigby arranged Brennan to lie naked in the centre of his bed with his hands above his head on the pillow. He clicked the cuff over his right wrist. He frowned at it. After a little bit of rummaging around along the headboard and dispensing with Brennan's pillow, Rigby discovered a metal support on the headboard. He looped the small length of chain behind it and deftly clicked the cuff around Brennan's left wrist.

He straightened up and looked Brennan over. "Damn, that's hot," he muttered. He touched

Brennan's cheek. "It would be even better if you'd look at me."

Brennan couldn't. Rigby would see too much in his eyes. Brennan let Rigby turn his head, but he didn't look up.

"If you're not actually into this after all then..." Rigby reached up to undo the cuffs.

"Please don't," Brennan said, trying to pull the cuffs out of Rigby's reach so he couldn't take his bondage away.

Rigby hesitated. He looked into Brennan's eyes for a moment before he could look away. "You're not just into this, you're *really* into this, aren't you? You're a... submissive?"

Brennan closed his eyes. He'd never had a problem with the label until he knew what it could mean for him and Rigby. Liking kink was one thing, liking it so much he couldn't demand that a dominant personality treat him with a bit of respect was an entirely different matter.

"This is what all that stuff about controlling the kiss was all about," Rigby went on. "It's not about who tops, it's about who gets the keys to the handcuffs."

Brennan forced himself to open his eyes. He forced himself to meet Rigby's gaze. He was just about to say Rigby could take the cuffs off if they weren't doing anything for him when he saw the expression in Rigby's face.

His eyes kept travelling over Brennan's body, hot and possessive and just a little bit intimidating for someone so used to the laughing, joking, best friend version of Rigby.

"You know those guys in clubs who might have been psychopaths—" Brennan began, wondering if his friend had more in common with them than he would have ever believed. In the back of his mind, a little voice said that it was probably a really stupid idea to introduce Rigby to kink when he was still getting used to a jealous side he'd apparently only just discovered.

Rigby put his finger over Brennan's lips. "No."

Brennan stopped speaking and raised an eyebrow.

"You don't talk about them," Rigby said, and took his finger away.

"I don't?" Brennan asked.

Rigby shook his head. He ran his hands over Brennan's chest. Pausing only to tweak Brennan's nipple and examine the responding gasp. "Whatever you did before the list doesn't count," Rigby announced.

"I hate to break it to you, Rig, but you really were the only one who lost their guy-on-guy virginity last night," Brennan managed to say, with something like his usual sarcasm.

"You don't talk about them. You don't think about them. As far as I'm concerned you never did anything else with another guy in your life," Rigby said firmly. "You're mine, and I have no intention of sharing any part of you with other guys—even your memories."

Brennan blinked at him. Where the hell had that come from? And more importantly, where could he get more of it?

"Mine," Rigby repeated.

"And do all your ex-girlfriends disappear as well?" Brennan asked, trying not to love the possessive side of Rigby too much, trying to keep even the vaguest sense of equality between them.

"What?" Rigby frowned. His hands trailed down to Brennan's stomach, so his fingers could outline each of his abs in turn. "They aren't important, they were just girls."

All of a sudden, Brennan wasn't sure Rigby was just talking about remembering girls. "So I'm a born again virgin and you still get to screw around?" he asked, no longer sure that point was as settled as he thought it was.

Rigby wrapped his hand around Brennan's cock. It was a very unfair but incredibly effective way to win an argument.

"I'm not screwing around behind your back, Bren. I'm just telling you, very politely, that you belong to me." He started to slowly stroke Brennan's erection.

Brennan squirmed on the bed, trying to ignore the stimulation and not thrust into Rigby's hand while they were supposed to be arguing.

"And since we both know damn well you like every word I've said to you on the subject, you can stop moaning about it," Rigby told him, with a hint of his usual bossy self.

Brennan nodded. He was quite willing to agree with anything Rigby said if it kept Rigby's hand on him and working him like that.

"Say it."

"Say what?" Brennan asked.

"Say you belong to me," Rigby ordered.

Brennan swallowed. He closed his eyes.

Rigby's hand never hesitated.

"I belong to you," Brennan said, whispering the words out loud for the first time. Somehow, right then, the words felt new, as if he hadn't belonged to Rigby for years.

"I don't ever want to have to go and fetch you from a bar again," Rigby said seriously. "If we go, we go together, and don't expect me to let you out of my sight."

Brennan nodded. He could live with that.

"I guess I belong to you in a way too," Rigby said softly.

Brennan blinked up at him.

Rigby grinned. "Don't get carried away, Bren. I might be somewhat soppy, but I'm not submissive. I'll leave that part of the game to you."

Brennan tried to study his friend and work out if Rigby thought about him any differently now. He knew a lot of men as strong and as dominant as Rigby wouldn't respect a submissive personality, no matter how much they enjoyed screwing one. Some men just couldn't give their respect to someone who didn't demand it, and Brennan didn't feel capable of demanding anything from Rigby right then.

Rigby smiled down at him. "I really don't know what's happened since we started all this," he said. "I've never been jealous over anyone before. I care more about you than anyone I ever dated."

"If you're going to say you love me like a brother, get your hand off my cock first," Brennan managed to say through gritted teeth. Rigby's hand still idly worked his erection.

"Definitely not feeling brotherly," Rigby confirmed. "But I do think I was half way in love with you before

I even realised I liked guys—which is actually one hell of an accomplishment for someone up to his ears in denial."

Brennan looked up at Rigby, trying to work out what the hell he was talking about.

"It's actually your fault I stayed in denial for so long too," Rigby informed Brennan, starting to twist his hand on every other upstroke.

"How do you work that out?" Brennan gasped. He tried to bend his knees up and plant his heels against the mattress so he could thrust up into Rigby's hand.

Rigby calmly rearranged his legs with his free hand, putting Brennan right back where he started.

"You were so sure about it all," Rigby said. "I thought if you were so sure you liked guys and not girls, then my quite liking girls had to mean I was straight. And..." his touch slowed.

Brennan looked up at him, trying to see the situation from Rigby's point of view. It was almost impossible for him to imagine not knowing exactly which way he swung. Brennan had always been so very sure.

"And I never had to feel jealous before. I knew you didn't care about any of the men you went to clubs with. What you said was right. You always came back to me. I had a boyfriend for years before I got around to having sex with men." He grinned. "You have no idea how many of my ex-girlfriends shouted that at me at one time or another—usually when I said I couldn't meet up with them because I had plans with you."

Brennan met Rigby's eyes. He looked so sure now, so sincere about every word.

Rigby's grin softened into a gentler smile. "Here's what we're going to do. I'm going to suck your cock. Then it's my turn to top. If you really can't live without an in depth conversation about what's going to happen between us in the future, we'll talk about that after we have sex. For now, these are the highlights—you belong to me. I, in a completely different way, belong to you. I'm bi, you're gay, and neither of us are going to screw anyone else. Any questions?"

Brennan shook his head.

Rigby leant over and kissed him. Brennan forced himself to at least make an effort and try to take control of the kiss.

It was kind of sweet that Brennan could be handcuffed naked to a bed and still think there was a chance he was going to be the one calling the shots. Rigby slid his free hand into Brennan's hair and held his head still, tilting it back to give him the perfect angle.

His other hand continued to slowly jack Brennan off. He felt amazing in Rigby's hand. Rigby leant back, breaking the kiss to look down Brennan's body. His cock was flushed with arousal and slicked with his pre-cum, sliding perfectly through his hand. More than that, the sense of control, of literally having his lover in the palm of his hand, was fantastically erotic. With the handcuffs and Brennan's submissive side thrown in, Rigby couldn't wish for anything more in a lover.

Brennan dropped his head back on the mattress and gasped for breath. Rigby stroked him a few more times as he shifted down the bed. He had the uncomfortable feeling a blow job wasn't something you could bluff your way through—not if he wanted to give Brennan as good a ride as Brennan gave him back in the pool.

"Tell me what you like?" he ordered.

Brennan blinked his eyes open and looked down at him. "Anything," he said. Rigby didn't think that was the emerging submissive side of Brennan talking. It sounded more like he just wasn't thinking clearly enough to give him any better advice.

Trial and error it was going to be then. Rigby steadied Brennan's cock with his fist and cautiously kissed the tip.

Brennan whimpered. He liked that. Rigby did it again. He trailed his lips over the sensitive glans again and again, he flicked his tongue out and tasted salt, but nothing much else.

Brennan moaned. Rigby grinned. Who needed instructions when he could get feedback like that? He wrapped his lips around the head, just taking the glans into his mouth. Looking up, he saw Brennan staring down at him, his jaw slack with pleasure.

He took a little more of Brennan's shaft in his mouth, but quickly pulled back. With any thoughts of deep throating his friend cast aside until he'd had a lot more practice, Rigby gave all his concentration to the head.

It didn't seem to take too long before he could feel Brennan's tension build to a sharp peak. Rigby pulled back and let Brennan's cock slip from his mouth.

"What..." Brennan gaped down at him. "Hand," he whispered.

Rigby had no idea what the random word meant.

"If… if you don't want to finish me with your month, use your hand," Brennan said. "Or undo the cuffs so I can, or…"

Rigby didn't need him to finish the sentence. He heard the desperation in Brennan's voice—do whatever you want, just please let me come.

"Don't worry, love, I'll take care of you. You've got lube, right?"

Brennan nodded quickly, catching up with why Rigby stopped. "Drawer," he whispered.

Rigby snagged lube and a condom out of the bed side cabinet. He added lube to his fingers. Brennan pulled his legs back, blatantly offering himself to his friend. Rigby had never seen anything more erotic in his life.

Slow. If he had learned one thing from Brennan topping him the night before it was he had to somehow manage to go slow. He slid his fingers gently against Brennan's tightly puckered hole and slowly slipped a finger inside his best friend. Brennan clamped down around him.

Rigby looked at his finger. There was no way anything bigger than his finger was ever going to fit inside an opening that tight. He cautiously moved his finger back and forth.

"Does that hurt?" he asked.

Brennan shook his head. "Feels good. Two."

"You said slow," Rigby reminded him.

"For you. Not my first time. Two fingers."

"We said we weren't going to talk about anything you did before," Rigby reminded him.

"You know what would really encourage me to shut up at this point?" Brennan asked, his familiar sarcastic spirit making a sudden return. "Two fingers."

Rigby frowned. He moved his finger back and forth some more. It really looked like two weren't going to fit.

"Rig, unless you want to hear all about what I did with every guy I've ever met..."

He whimpered as Rigby quickly slid another lube slick finger inside him alongside the first one. Brennan pushed himself back against Rigby's fingers. Rigby watched, mesmerised as his finger disappeared and reappeared again and again, somehow fitting in a space which couldn't possibly take them.

Moments passed. "Three," Brennan demanded.

Rigby was past the point of demanding slow. If Brennan was ready, he wasn't going to argue. He added an extra coat of slickness to his fingers and stretched Brennan's hole wide open around three digits.

"Condom and cock," Brennan demanded.

Rigby didn't need telling twice.

He rolled the latex down his shaft, smeared the condom with lube and leaned over Brennan.

"Now," Brennan told him.

"I thought I was supposed to be the bossy one," Rigby whispered against his lips as he stole a kiss.

He didn't give Brennan time to answer before he slid into him. Brennan's eyes dropped closed, his lips parted with pure pleasure.

"Mine," Rigby demanded.

Brennan blinked his eyes open. His hands pulled at the cuffs as he squirmed under Rigby's body, trying to make his lover move inside him. "Yours," he whispered, finally realising Rigby wasn't going to move until he said it.

Rigby looked into his eyes and he could tell the other man really meant that word.

"Mine," he whispered back again. He stole whatever else Brennan would have said with a kiss and began to carefully thrust into Brennan's arse.

He was so tight, and so perfect, Rigby knew it would all be over far too soon. If it was over before he managed to work out how to find Brennan's prostate with his cock, it was all going to be very embarrassing.

Rigby caught Brennan's legs on the inside of his elbows and pushed them back to his chest, opening him further. The angle changed. Brennan gave a half scream and clamped down around him again and again as his semen splattered against their chests on the first solid contact between prostate and cock.

Brennan's clenching hole took Rigby over the edge with him. He thrust hard and fast into his friend until he only had enough strength to half collapse on top of him, barely able to keep any of his weight off Brennan's body.

Brennan murmured contentedly underneath him.

"I'll move in a moment," Rigby reassured him.

Brennan hummed a response, but he didn't seem particularly concerned about being half crushed underneath him. Rigby gradually built up the energy to roll off him. He looked Brennan over—he was so sleepy and heavy lidded, he barely stirred as Rigby cleaned them up. He just blinked up at Rigby, so serene and trusting, so beautiful.

Rigby stole a quick kiss and tried to lie down next to him, but Brennan wouldn't move over. He gave a sleepy chuckle and looked above his head. Rigby followed his gaze to the cuffs. He undid them and Brennan kindly moved over to let him into the bed.

Brennan kept his gaze down, not quite meeting Rigby's eyes. When Rigby finally convinced him to look up, all he got was a shy little smile. Rigby switched the light off and arranged them so they could spoon comfortably together for the night, cuddling close in a way that won't make any limbs fall asleep before they did.

"Rig?"

"Yes?" he asked, pulling Brennan closer still.

"How long do you think it will take to finish the new to do list you made?"

"Forever."

Brennan shook his head. "I'm not asking you to be soppy about it, I just… I just want a ball park figure in my head so I can—" he trailed off. With a shrug he finally settled on an end to the sentence a few minutes later. "So I can relax for a while without thinking the list will be finished any minute. I think that will let me deal with it all."

"It will take forever," Rigby said more firmly. "Because if I ever run out of things to add to the end of the list, we're going to start back again at the beginning and do it all over again." Rigby held him tighter still. "You belong to me now, Bren. Understand? That's not going to change."

Brennan shook his head.

"That's not going to change," Rigby repeated.

Brennan still didn't relax.

Rigby switched on the light and grabbed the new list he started making off the bed side table. "When there is anything on this list that isn't crossed off, you still belong to me," he said. "And what I said about me adding things to the list all the time to make sure that's always true still stands, okay?"

Brennan looked at the list for a while, then he shifted slightly in Rigby's arms. This time it felt more like he was making himself comfortable rather than getting ready to flee.

"That's a really stupid idea," Brennan announced with a last glance at the list.

Rigby grinned. The familiar accusation was all the agreement he ever needed to hear from his friend. They knew any further sarcasm, any further protest, would just be made out of habit and for the sake of appearances. The real decision had already been made.

Rigby moved to put the list back on the bedside table, but at the last moment he changed his mind. Grabbing his pen, he rested the notebook on Brennan's shoulder began to scrawl an addition at the bottom of the list.

"What are you doing?" Brennan asked, craning his neck to try and see what he was writing.

"Stay still," he said. "You're making the paper wobble."

Brennan gave a long suffering sigh but did as Rigby wanted for a few moments.

Careful to make sure his friend couldn't see what he'd written, Rigby put the list back on the bedside table and once more tried to arrange them both comfortably for the night.

"You really think I'm going to sleep before you tell me what you wrote?" Brennan asked.

"You can read it in the morning."

"I can also keep talking and wriggling all through the night," Brennan pointed out. "Or at least until you give up and let me see what you added to the list—whichever comes first."

Rigby rolled his eyes heavenward, realising Brennan would actually do that if he didn't get his own way. He retrieved the list and handed it over.

Brennan read the new note at the bottom of the list.

Tell Brennan I'm in love with him.

Brennan swallowed. He glanced at Rigby, and then back to the paper. His eyes went back and forth across that same line of messy handwriting over and over again. Rigby held his breath, suddenly nervous about how his friend might react to the declaration.

Taking the pen out of Rigby's hand, Brennan added a few neatly written words of his own to the end on the list. He reached past Rigby and put the note book and the pen on the bedside table.

Tell Rigby I love him too.

Brennan cleared his throat, his cheeks flushed hot with embarrassment. He wouldn't meet Rigby's eye, but he relaxed in his arms. For the first time, he seemed to realise that was exactly where he belonged.

Rigby nodded to himself, pleased that he'd finally found a way to get his message across. He switched the light off and smiled quietly to himself in the darkness, imagining all the other things they could start to tick off the list the following morning. And in the morning after that. And during all the mornings, afternoons and evenings to come.

There was no rush. After all, they had plenty of time to do everything that either of them could add on to the list. They had forever.

About the Author

Kim is 25 years old, from a small town in South Wales.

After writing for years, Kim is finally editing some of the stories to share with the rest of the world. Kim writes both male/male and male/female stories that range from the dark and paranormal right through to the lighter, funnier side of life.

The only thing every story contains is a happy ever after for the two (or more!) characters that deserve it most. Oh, and kinky sex — there's always plenty of that too — but Kim takes no responsibility for any of that. It's all the characters' fault. Honest…

Kim Dare loves to hear from readers. You can find her contact information, website details and author profile page at http://www.total-e-bound.com

Total-E-Bound Publishing

www.total-e-bound.com

Take a look at our exciting range of literagasmic™
erotic romance titles and discover pure quality
at Total-E-Bound.